# *The*
# PEARL HARBOR MURDERS

# *The*
# PEARL HARBOR MURDERS

## MAX ALLAN COLLINS

BERKLEY PRIME CRIME, NEW YORK

THE PEARL HARBOR MURDERS

A Berkley Prime Crime Book / published by arrangement with the author

ISBN: 0-7394-1715-0

Berkley Prime Crime Books are published by The Berkley Publishing Group, a division of Penguin Putnam Inc., 375 Hudson Street, New York, New York 10014. The name BERKLEY PRIME CRIME and the BERKLEY PRIME CRIME design are trademarks belonging to Penguin Putnam Inc.

PRINTED IN THE UNITED STATES OF AMERICA

*In memory of my father—*
*Max A. Collins, Sr.—*
*who served in the Pacific*

Though this work is fanciful, an underpinning of history supports the events depicted in these pages. The author intends no disrespect for the real people who inspired the characterizations herein, nor to take lightly that day of infamy.

"This week a high officer of the U.S. Army remarked that he knows of no place under the American flag safer than Hawaii—more secure from the onslaught of actual war."

—*Honolulu Star Bulletin,* May 1941

"There is no chivalry in complete war."

—Edgar Rice Burroughs

# ONE:

*December 5, 1941*

# ONE

## *Boat Day*

In less than forty-eight hours, six Japanese aircraft carriers—220 miles north of the island of Oahu—would launch 350 warplanes in an attack not preceded by any formal declaration of war. Every significant Naval and air installation would feel the brunt of the surprise raid, which lasted less than two hours and cost the United States military three destroyers, three cruisers, eight auxiliary craft, eight battleships, 188 aircraft and the lives of 1,763 officers and men. This figure increased to 2,404 when fatalities ashore—including civilian—were added to the grim roster.

To the survivors, these deaths seemed more like murder than casualties of war: the unsuspecting victims on the *Arizona,* a thousand sailors on a single battleship obliterated by a single bomb during peacetime, were victims of a sneak attack one historian aptly termed as "outside the bounds of traditional warfare . . . better described as mass murder."

The first of these Pearl Harbor murders, however, took place not on December 7, but in the predawn hours of December 6 . . . a murder that might have been an early warning signal, had it been properly heeded.

Making sense of the inherently senseless act of murder is never an easy task; but two men tried, a father and son, and this is their story.


Hully (short for Hulbert) Burroughs found Honolulu very much to his liking. At thirty-two, a leanly muscular six-footer with an oval, boyishly handsome face and a shock of dark hair, Hully found this tropical town an excellent place for a gainfully employed young bachelor to spend an extended vacation. .

When he had first arrived, in September, Hully—perhaps reduced to a child again, in his father's presence—had all but raced to the Aloha Tower, adjacent to where his steamer, the S. S. *Mariposa,* had docked. His pop had humored him, tagging along to the white ten-foot Art Moderne tower with its four looming clock dials, going up the self-service elevator to the observation deck, open to the sky, a view on every side.

Looking toward the open sea, Hully took in a vista that included a harbor channel dotted with small and large craft, powered by sail or motor. At the west, toward Pearl Harbor, a Dole cannery water tower painted to resemble a huge pineapple rose absurdly above green cane fields, like a World's Fair pavilion. Looking east, toward Waikiki, frond-flung boulevards pointed to Diamond Head. And looking inland, north, he could note the low-slung cityscape of red-tiled roofs and tin-awning-shaded stores rising in tandem with palm trees, pink stucco structures providing pale smears of color amid stark blossoms of red, white and blue; he could see, too, like pyramids piercing an oasis, the austere limestone edifices of the trading houses and banks of the Caucasian (*haole*) upper class . . . and the grandly, even ridiculously rococo Iolani Palace . . . and the Nuuanu Valley, hugged by the ridges and slopes of the Koolau range. . . .

He had soon come to know Honolulu as the tiny colonial city it was, a low-key paradise where your wake-up call was courtesy of a mynah bird, where you drifted down to a white beach for a sunrise swim, where the workdays were short and the evenings endless.

His father, not surprisingly, took a less romantic view: what O. B.—"Old Burroughs," the nickname Hully, his brother Jack and sister Joan all used for their father, after he took to signing his letters to them that way—saw as Hawaii's appeal was the casual island atmosphere, white sandy beaches and local dress that ran to untucked shirt, shorts and sandals.

At sixty-six, Hully's pop could have passed for fifty, a rugged man's man, with laughing squinty blue eyes set in a poker face the same oval shape as Hully's, only without the dark hair on top: the old man was bald but for iron-gray bristles at his temples. Ed Burroughs had long been a devout sunbather, and was tanned to a rich bronze worthy of Tarzan himself.

Which was fitting, because Hully's father was Edgar Rice Burroughs, who was also the father of Tarzan, "the best-known literary character of the twentieth century," according to a recent issue of *The Saturday Evening Post*. That same magazine had dubbed the unpretentious novelist who created the famed apeman "the world's greatest living writer" . . . an irony Hully's pop bitterly savored, since the *Post* had rejected every story he had ever sent them, including one after the publication of that laudatory article.

It was a few minutes past noon, and Hully and his father were once again at the dock, seeing off friends who were boarding the fabled Great White Ship of the Matson Line, the S. S. *Lurline*. Normally, his pop—who disliked crowds—would have disdained Honolulu's famed Boat Day, with its mobbed pier, its barrage of streamers, its confetti snowstorm.

Pop even rejected the delightfully swaying hips of hula girls, and Hully could well understand why his dad loathed the din of the strumming ukuleles of beachboys serenading women they'd seduced combined with the blare of the Royal Hawaiian Band.

Some of these brown-as-a-berry local boys were diving for coins from the top decks.

"Buster Crabbe used to do that," Hully reminded his father teasingly. Beachboy Buster had been an Olympic star before going to Hollywood.

"Maybe he made a good beachboy," O. B. said. "But he was still a lousy Tarzan."

Due to fear of war with Japan, the dock was more heavily guarded than ever before. The authorities—and the *haole* citizenry—were well aware that 40 percent of Hawaii's population was Japanese; so the nationalized Hawaii Territorial Guard had been called out. Of course, the Guard was primarily made up of Japanese. . . .

It seemed to Hully that the women at the dock today greatly outnumbered the men—military wives, most likely, being sent to the mainland because their husbands suspected the coming war with Japan would soon restrict travel from Hawaii to California. But it wasn't all men: as usual, politicians and businessmen were among the masses, making deals, trading gossip.

This Boat Day crowd ran well into the thousands, though only eight hundred passengers were departing; and this was typical. Matson Line calendars, marking days of departure and arrival, hung in kitchens and businesses all over Honolulu, and many a housewife and downtown office worker regularly left their respective stations to join in on the Boat Day festivities.

"Looks like a goddamn ice-cream-salesman convention," his pop had grumbled, referring to the overbearing, sun-reflective whiteness of the crowd's attire—females in white cotton dresses shaded by white parasols, Naval officers in dress whites. Like so many civilian males here today, the Burroughses themselves were in white linen suits—no shorts and sandals for Boat Day—and white Panama hats. Pop had his Panama brim snugged down, so as not to be recognized.

His dad didn't mind doing publicity—he often posed on the set of the MGM Tarzan pictures, with Hollywood's current apeman, Johnny Weissmuller—when it was structured, a part of his work. When he went out socially, he abhorred the kind of attention the local reporters would stick him with, if they spotted him.

Typically, Pop had lain back when Hully escorted Marjorie to the gangway, knowing that the photographers would be snapping at her heels like hungry dogs. Marjorie Petty—who for the last five glorious weeks Hully had been dating—was the daughter of pinup artist George Petty; she was, in fact, a living Petty Girl right out of the pages of *Esquire,* since she was her father's model.

It had been an innocent romance, a few kisses exchanged under the gold moon in a purple sky. But Marjorie—enjoying a Hawaiian vacation as a college graduation present—was almost constantly chaperoned by her mother (Petty's previous model), who looked somewhat askance upon the ten-year age difference between the Petty girl and the Burroughs boy.

Hully had dared a kiss before she boarded—for once, her mother didn't frown—and, a spring in his step, the young Burroughs rejoined his father, who was standing with the friend he was seeing off, the reason Tarzan's (and Hully's) daddy had braved the Boat Day crowd.

Colonel Frank Teske of the Army Signal Corps had already seen his wife and infant son aboard to their first-class stateroom, and had returned to invite the Burroughses to join them for refreshments till the "all ashore" was sounded.

"No thanks," the elder Burroughs said in his husky baritone, as Hully fell in beside him. "I'm off the sauce, and, anyway, I couldn't take those corridors reeking with damn leis, it's like dimestore perfume . . . not to mention the cigarette smoke."

Pop had quit drinking and smoking recently, and was of late displaying a reformer's intolerance for the second habit, if not for the first. As for the leis, personally Hully got a charge of the full, fragrant ropes of yellow ilima, the sweet-scented loops of mountain maile; not bad for a quarter apiece.

Colonel Teske was only one of many friends Hully's pop had in military circles. O. B. relished the army bustle of Fort DeRussy, Fort Ruger, Fort Shafter, and Schofield Barracks; a flier himself, he took any excuse for a trip over to Hickam Field. As for the Navy at Pearl Harbor, the elder Burroughs had on the very day Hully arrived taken his youngest boy to Battleship Row for a personal tour of the *California,* courtesy of its captain.

Hully had soon learned that his father was thick with most of the brass on Oahu—Hawaii was easy duty for officers, who had lots of time on their hands, and were more than willing to mix with civilians, particularly one as famous as Hully's pop.

Thirtyish, a knife blade of a man with a pencil mustache, just another white linen suit in the crowd, Colonel Teske said, "I appreciate you coming down like this, Ed. I'm sure going to miss our poker games."

"I'm going to miss winning your money," O. B. said.

In the shadow of his own Panama, the colonel's eyes were tight, and he spoke so softly his words barely registered above the din. "I only wish you'd take my advice and get the hell back to the mainland."

"Come on, Frank," O. B. replied, in his typical staccato fashion. "You know a Jap attack here is a long shot. This entire island is a fortress! Every point, every headland fortified . . . Navy and Army and Navy Air Corps, twenty-five thousand troops! I refuse to worry."

"Get yourself on the next boat, Ed."

A smirk dimpled Burroughs' cheek. "Well, if a skinflint like you springs for traveling first class, you must mean what you say."

Shaking his head, Teske said, "First Class was the only accommodation available. There's a record number of passengers on this trip—seventy of 'em assigned to cots in the main lounge!"

O. B. pawed the air goodnaturedly with a big blunt hand. "I don't deny war's coming. But Honolulu is one of the safest places under the Flag. Teske, you're a damn pessimist!"

Hully wasn't so sure he agreed with his father. After all, the *Matsonia*—the *Lurline*'s sister ship—had been recently converted to a troopship; today was the first time in two weeks transportation to California had been available, excluding a few seats on the Pan Am clippers.

"No offense, Colonel," Hully said, "but you told us there'd be an attack by Thanksgiving, and nothing happened. What makes you think—"

"You'll probably be all right till Christmas. Oh hell, who knows?" Teske put a hand on O. B.'s shoulder. "You may be right, Ed—or why else would the brass order me to San Francisco?"

"What are you doing, heading out there, Colonel?" Hully asked. "If you can say . . ."

"Same thing I was supposed to be doing here—install radar installations, and run simulated attacks by carrier-based planes."

"Now *that* makes sense," Burroughs said. "The San Francisco Navy Yard, there's a target."

Teske shrugged. "Anyway, I'm glad to get out of this madhouse. . . . Ed, thanks for the send-off. I'll see you in the States."

"One of these days," Burroughs said.

Father and son did not wait around for the *Lurline*'s actual departure, avoiding the hoopla of whistle blasts and a brassy "Aloha Oe," hoping to beat the crowd. They had parked three blocks away, noting more police in evidence than usual—further sabotage fear?—and Fort and Bishop streets were jammed with traffic; it was getting as bad as back home in California, Hully thought.

Pop drove, as usual—he loved to drive—and they both tossed their Panamas on the floor in the backseat, as otherwise the wind would have whisked the hats away; the top was down on the sporty white '37 Pierce Arrow, a twelve-cylinder with chrome wheel covers. They were heading Waikiki way along the Ala Moana (Sea Road), and traffic had let up some.

As they glided by the United States Army Transport docks, across from which was the Hawaiian General Depot and the Air Depot, Hully asked, "What exactly does Colonel Teske do?"

His blacksmith's hands gripping the steering wheel,

O. B. glanced over at his son, blue eyes hard. "Besides talk a lot of pessimistic baloney? He's with the Army Signal Corps. Commander of the Army's aircraft warning system in Hawaii."

Hully had not been privy to the conversations between Teske and his father, but he knew the colonel had arrived only about a month ago, and was a recent addition to the roster of his pop's military pals.

"So what's this about radar?" Hully asked. They were passing the Myrtle and Healani Boat Clubs.

"Well, you know what it is, don't you?"

"Sure."

"Frank brought radar to the islands, and it's a damn good idea, too. Look at the role it played in the Battle of Britain." O. B. shrugged, wind whipping the white linen of his jacket. "And I guess I can't blame Frank for his attitude—both the military *and* the civilians have given him one load of horseshit after another."

"How so?"

"Well, General Short thinks mobile radar stations aren't worth operating on a twenty-four-hour basis. To him, they're just a good training tool for the lower ranks."

Rather enjoying the wind rustling his hair, Hully asked, "What good does radar do if you're not using it all the time?"

"None—that's Frank's point."

Just ahead was the entrance to Fort Armstrong, one of five Coast Artillery Defense Batteries on Oahu.

"You said civilians were giving him crap, too," Hully said. "What do civilians have to do with it?"

"Plenty, when it's the governor. Him, and the National Park Service. They won't let Frank put his radar setups on mountain peaks, where they'd be most effective—it might ruin the view."

"Hell," Hully said, snorting a laugh. "I can see why Colonel Teske is frustrated."

"So can I, son, but he's still wrong about a Japanese air raid on Oahu. And most military personnel, and informed civilians, agree with me, in considering that a remote possibility."

They were nearing Kewalo Basin, home of sampans in the water and out—several Japanese boatbuilding firms sat along the artificial harbor with its fleet of marine-blue sampans, blending with the water they bobbed in.

"The threat here," his father said, casting an eye toward the man-made Japanese harbor, "isn't from above—it's from within."

"Sabotage."

He nodded, his expression grave, his thick hands tight on the wheel. "I know you don't agree with me on this, Hully, but you can't deny the reality—better than one out of three Hawaiians are of Jap heritage."

"Come on, O. B.—the majority of them are hard-working, conservative souls—"

"With relatives living back in Japan," his father finished. "A good number of these *issei* and *nisei* are Japanese citizens. . . ."

*Issei* were first-generation immigrants, ineligible for U.S. citizenship, and *nisei* were born in Hawaii, and as such were U.S. citizens.

Trying to rein in his irritation, Hully said, "The *nisei* hold dual citizenships, Pop. You know that."

O. B. frowned over at his son. "Yes, and if war breaks out, what flag will they serve under?"

Hully gave his dad a sarcastic smile. "And I suppose you think sweet Mrs. Fujimoto is just waiting for a signal from the homeland to slit our throats in the night."

The junior Burroughs was referring to their efficient, kindly, obviously loyal maid, who happened to be the mother of a friend of Hully's; it was his close friendship with a *nisei* that had got these occasional near arguments going between father and son.

Despite the absurdity of it, O. B. said, "How do you know she isn't? How do you know your friend Sam won't stab you in the back?"

"Because he's my friend, Dad."

This was an old argument, and father and son fell into an awkward silence, punctuated by the whistle of wind and the flaglike flapping of white linen.

Along this stretch of the Ala Moana, a fantastic, breathtaking view presented itself, including Punch Bowl and Round Top and Tantalus and Kaimuki and Diamond Head, the tower of the Royal Hawaiian Hotel peeking over the tops of coconut and date palms like a kid over a fence.

Finally Hully said, "Jeez, Pop, I never saw so many women in one place in my life, as on that dock today."

His father nodded.

"Wives of servicemen, mostly, I suppose," Hully said.

"Some of 'em. Most of them were prostitutes."

Hully, not sure his father was serious, looked at him, saying, "What? Really?"

But O. B.'s expression was matter-of-fact; so was his tone. "Sure. And that's the only thing that makes me think Frank Teske might not be entirely nuts."

"Why is that?"

"Well, when the prostitutes around a military base panic, and start headin' for the mainland, you gotta wonder—who is more sensitive to the military mind than a hooker?"

They were rumbling across a long wooden bridge over the Ala Moana Canal, which emptied the city's waste water into the ocean. Their lodgings would be coming up soon, and when the wind blew from the south, no one went down to the hotel's beach to swim— at such times O. B. tended to refer to the otherwise comfortable Niumalu Hotel as "Hovel-on-Sewer."

Soon they were passing what appeared to be an old Southern mansion set stylishly among the lush shrubbery; but it was actually a Japanese teahouse called Ikesu Villa.

"Take that place," O. B. said with a nod. "It looks American, but it's Japanese through and through."

Shortly after, at a fork in the road, Hully's father turned right, into that part of Waikiki which still most nearly remained in its native state.

"You know," O. B. said reflectively, the antagonism suddenly gone from his voice, "the funny thing is . . . this is as close as I've ever been to war. I've always been the kind of guy who's late for the thrill—I always seem to get to the fire after it's out."

Hully took a long sideways look at his rugged, bronzed father—a man's man who had been a cowboy and a gold miner, who had served the United States Cavalry in Arizona, who had sailed the Panama Canal.

But who—as the creator of Tarzan—had never been to Africa, and not so long ago, when MGM announced its next Weissmuller epic would be shot on the Dark Continent, Hully's pop had been invited to accompany the expedition . . . only the war in Europe and Africa had changed all that. Africa was off.

"And now I'm too old," his father was saying, wheeling into and up the Niumalu's crushed coral drive. "One last war, and I'm too damn old."

For the first time in several weeks, Hully heard the familiar despondency in his father's voice, reminding him why he'd come here for this "vacation"—a fear in his family that his father might be contemplating suicide.

And wasn't that ironic, Hully thought: what a Japanese thing for O. B. to be considering.

# TWO

## *A Nazi at the Niumalu*

The mile of romance, the Tourist Bureau called it: that white stretch of sand known as Waikiki, extending from the Halekulani Hotel and the adjacent inns and cottages to the concrete War Memorial Natatorium in whose saltwater pool that former screen Tarzan, Buster Crabbe, had set records, warming up for the Olympics.

Only one major beachfront hotel rested outside those limits, sequestered from the rest of Waikiki by Fort de Russy: the Niumalu, literally Spreading Coconut, loosely Sheltering Palms, of which the lavishly land-scaped grounds, six acres' worth, certainly had their share . . . and the hotel's hand-lettered sign was rather informally nailed to one leaning palm, establishing a casual tone that permeated the place.

Thirty clapboard guest cottages were scattered about the Niumalu's pleasant jungle, with all crushed-coral roads leading to an impressive if squatty-looking white stucco main building typical of the Hawaiian style of architecture prevalent since the late twenties, with its lampshadelike double-pitched roof, and a porte cochere supported by columns of lava stone evocative of leopard spots.

The lodge, as the guests referred to the central building, had an open interior with a central rock-garden courtyard just off a nightclublike dining room with a large dance floor and bandstand. The lobby's large, missionlike arched portals also looked out onto the courtyard, and the effect was open and airy, the wicker furnishings adding to a porchlike effect.

Edgar Rice Burroughs had been very happy here, with his wife Florence—his second wife—and he had thought she felt the same.

Burroughs had well known the risks of marrying a younger woman. He had been sixty and Florence thirty-one—as his daughter Joan had cruelly pointed out, Florence was younger than the duration of her parents' marriage. Everyone seemed to be making the assumption that he was discarding his fifty-nine-year-old, overweight wife for the slender shapely former actress, out of the usual crassly selfish, male, sex-driven reasons.

The truth was more complex. Emma had always been plump, pleasantly so in her young, vivacious days, a "dumpling," as the old parlance went. In the early years of the marriage, even as her tendency toward stoutness increased, her intelligence and charm had made up for her excess weight. After all, they had faced hardship, poverty and adversity together; theirs had been a marriage of closeness, of sharing. Emma would read his work and intelligently comment; his triumphs, his failures, had been hers—theirs, Jane to his Tarzan.

But their interests had diverged, drastically, over the past twenty years. Emma seemed to resent his youthful ways, shared not at all his interest in sports and the great out-of-doors—horseback riding, golf, tennis, certainly not flying. She would chastise him for his preference for the company of younger people, calling him "immature," accusing him of trying to "prove his masculinity."

The latter, in a marriage that had been sexless for some time, was a particularly cutting blow. But—despite the quarrels, and the recriminations—he had held on, out of concern for how his children might react to separation or divorce. With his business flourishing, he spent less and less time at home, doing his writing at the office, supervising the magazine serialization of his work, keeping an eye on the licensing of Tarzan and other characters of his to the movies, radio, and comics.

And all of this was rewarding—he thought of himself as a businessman first, a writer second, an "author" not at all. He had been the first writer he knew of to incorporate—ERB, Inc.—and even started a publishing company, printing his own books, to better maintain control of the product, and to maximize profits.

And he had made it a family business, hiring Hully as his vice president, using his older son, Jack, a successful commercial artist, as the illustrator of his book jackets and the new "John Carter of Mars" comic strip, based on his science-fiction novels, set to debut this Sunday. He'd even hired his daughter's no-good husband Jim Pierce to play Tarzan on the radio.

No one could say Ed Burroughs was not a family man, even if he did spend most of his time away from home, at the office. But few on this earth knew—besides his children, if they would admit it—how he had dreaded to come home, at the end of a long day. And even the kids could only guess that behind the happy moments of the marriage—and there had been some, even in the later years—hovered a specter of fear of what he knew would inevitably come the next day or the next. . . .

He blamed himself. He'd always been proud of the way he could hold his liquor, and had urged Emma—who had no tolerance for alcohol at all, and whose personality changed radically under the influence—to moderate her drinking. They had been party goers for years, but as Emma's problem worsened, he had cut back on the invitations they accepted, and didn't stay long at the parties they did attend.

And so Emma had begun to drink at home. Alone—in secret, that open secret the families of all alcoholics know too well.

He never knew what condition he would find her in—she might be in a vicious state or a comatose one. Whatever the case, countless hours of hideous suffering for both of them followed. Once he flew into a rage and dumped all of her liquor into the swimming pool—of course, since it had no filtration system, the pool had probably only benefited from the alcohol's sterilizing effect.

He had never wished to make Emma unhappy. But he could not overlook how horribly unhappy she had made him; she treated her pet dog more kindly. Ten years before he left her, Emma had said to him that she no longer liked him—for some reason, those simple words had inflicted a wound that had never healed.

Many people—friends and strangers alike, their appetites for the misfortunes of others fed by lice like Walter Winchell and other low-life gossipmongers—assumed his relationship with Florence preceded, even initiated, the breakup with Emma.

It was true he'd known Florence for some years, had admired her at a distance (she was the wife of a friend, the producer of his ill-fated Tarzan movie, which he'd backed as an antidote to the unfaithful MGM versions of his work). He'd felt unrequited schoolboy pangs of love for her, before she even knew he existed.

With her fair, curly hair, and her apple-cheeked wholesome beauty, Florence had been a popular child actress in the silent-movie days, a second Mary Pickford with a series of two-reelers for Mack Sennett leading to starring roles in features. When talkies came in, she had begun to raise a family with her producer husband, Ashton Dearholt, that good friend of Burroughs.

But Burroughs and Florence had been thrown together when his own separation was quickly followed by Florence's husband throwing her over—for an actress he had met on the Guatemala film shoot of the ill-starred Tarzan picture! Hell, even Burroughs

wouldn't have dared put together a plot so contrived—
but, like two lost souls, he and Florence had drifted
together.

That Florence and Burroughs's daughter Joan had
been good friends made the awkward situation ever
more strained. Hully and Jack, who had witnessed their
mother's alcoholic madness, understood far better, and
tried to make peace, but Joan avoided him, for years,
and never spoke to Florence again.

Perhaps it was inevitable that he and Florence would
wind up in Hawaii—they had honeymooned there, delightfully, in 1935. But his return to Oahu in 1940 had
been in part financially motivated. The pulp magazines—his major serialization market—had lowered
their pay rates, due to the squeeze of the Depression,
and the European war cut off most of his foreign markets. In Hawaii, he could drop his expenses to a third
of what they'd been in California.

His financial state, too, he knew was his own damn
fault—despite his businesslike attitudes toward writing,
he was lousy at managing money, and he knew it—
anyway, he knew it now. From buying the Tarzana
Ranch back in 1919—since sold off for subdivided
lots, his precious unspoiled land turned into another
goddamn suburb—to the acquisition of cars, horses,
and planes, Burroughs was a classic case of a man
living beyond his means.

Considering his earnings over the last thirty years,
the creator of Tarzan should have been poised for
wealthy retirement. Instead, he was an aging small
businessman supporting three grown children, an ex-

wife, a new wife and her two children, as well as an executive secretary and stenographer back in California, not to mention a Japanese maid in Hawaii.

Florence had always said that his fame was not what attracted her to him; she spoke of his self-deprecatory sense of humor, and the "fun and games" of his life, the outdoor sports, parties, dinner and theater. And in the first five years of their marriage, every evening seemed to begin—and, often, end—with cocktails at their own Rodeo Drive home or someone else's. On the rare night the couple wasn't making the restaurant/club/theater circuit, they were up till all hours playing backgammon, bridge, or mah-jongg with movie-star friends.

He'd always been an early riser, but the dazzle of a young wife and the bright lights of Southern California had seduced him into turning his schedule upside down—and his writing, the quantity and the quality, suffered accordingly.

Perhaps he had tried too hard to keep up with his young wife, burning the candle at both ends, and she eventually accused him of trying so hard to act youthfully that he had instead behaved childishly. In Hawaii, he had planned to crawl in and curl up in a hole to write, and pull the hole in after him—but Honolulu was an even bigger party town than Beverly Hills, and when he wasn't playing poker into the wee hours with his Army and Navy friends, he and his wife were at a luau or a cocktail party or off yachting.

Florence complained that she had turned into his chauffeur, since he was inevitably too tipsy to drive

home after a soiree, and felt she had fallen into the role
of the serious, "older" partner, while he was the child.

Since his Hawaiian writing was going well—by the
end of 1940, he'd written not only a new Tarzan novel
but entries in his other two mainstay series, Mars and
Pellucidar, with a Venus tale in the works—Burroughs
didn't think the nights of revelry were hurting anything.

Still, Florence began complaining, not only about his
"immaturity," but the Niumalu (one of the nicest hotels
on Oahu) which she found lacking, condemning it as
"cramped, buggy and damp." She was dismayed when
he told her they would be living on $250 a month, the
salary he was drawing from ERB, Inc.

Five years ago, she had viewed him as a dapper,
prosperous, respected gentleman, a father figure; now,
he feared, she saw him as just another bald, overweight
geezer.

Of course Florence's major complaint had been his
drinking, which led to full-blown arguments, like the
time she found he was keeping a carton of liquor under
the bed, for easy access. She claimed he was "drunk"
every night, and—worst of all—she said her children
were afraid of him, that he was "taking it out" on them.

This he greatly resented. He loved her two kids as
if they were his own, nine-year-old Caryl especially,
the little charmer. It was true he was harder on eleven-
year-old Lee, trying to urge the boy to be more athletic.
Florence claimed Lee was afraid of him—though he'd
never laid a hand on the child—and that he was showing his irritation to both kids, "acting up," she called
it.

When she packed up, gathering the two children, and announced she was leaving—when was it . . . eight months ago?—he could scarcely believe it. He had thought Florence's threats were empty, but—as they'd had a premarital understanding that should things not work out, either could "call it off" without objection from the other—he merely escorted them, numbly, to the *Lurline* at the dock, a shell-shocked zombie among the Boat Day festivities.

Nothing had ever hit him so hard. He found it bitterly, ironically amusing that Florence had left him because he was an obese drunk. . . . How Emma would have relished that.

His carousing ways ceased. He developed a routine of going to a movie and then to bed early, declining all invitations for poker and parties. He went for days without speaking to anyone, taking his meals in his bungalow, burrowed behind drawn blackout curtains. Despite this deep despondency, he did manage to keep writing, a historical yarn about the Romans, and he finished his Venus tale.

His only break from this self-imposed incarceration was a painful stay at Queen's Hospital, due to the flaring up of an old bladder condition. For three weeks he was shot full of derivatives of the poppy flower, fed an anesthetic that burned from his lips down his throat into his lungs, got filled full of sulfathiazole until he thought it would run out of his ears, and had a wire inserted in his favorite organ.

Upon his release, he began to imagine he was having small strokes and heart attacks, but didn't much care.

He felt he was going to die. He wondered if maybe helping that process along wasn't worth considering.

A note accompanying a revision of his will—in which he thanked his loyal secretary Ralph Rothmund for his longtime friendship, telling him what a pleasure it had been to work with him—apparently got his three children worrying about his mental state, alone on this Pacific island, and Hully had come to his rescue.

God bless that kid, claiming this was a "vacation."

They had moved into new digs near the beach at the Niumalu, a bedroom with bath and sitting room (Hully bunking it on a hideaway couch). Burroughs picked up the pace of his writing, even as he and his son enjoyed late, leisurely breakfasts, long lunches, afternoons of driving, horseback riding, fishing, sunbathing and, most of all, tennis.

He and Hully—and Jack, too, for that matter—had always enjoyed a friendly rivalry, where sports were concerned . . . swimming, riding, wrestling, tennis. Maybe Florence considered him immature, but Burroughs preferred "young at heart," and enjoyed trying to keep pace with his athletic offspring.

Hully had extended the friendly competition to quitting drinking, and losing weight. Burroughs knew his son feared his father was becoming an alcoholic, and privately had his own fears in that regard. So he had quit—and quit smoking, as well. Hully was down to 177 pounds, a loss of ten, and Burroughs had dropped sixteen pounds, down to 182.

After getting back from seeing Frank Teske off, the father and son had eaten a light lunch in the Niumalu dining room, after which Burroughs headed into the bungalow, to get some writing done—he needed to get his hero, Carson Napier, out of one jam and into another. He and Hully would play a round of tennis in the late afternoon on the court on the Niumalu grounds—Burroughs had prevailed yesterday, two sets to one . . . a spirited game that had exhausted him, though he was damned if he'd let his boy know just how tired he was.

In the sitting room with its pale plaster walls, near a churning window fan, Burroughs was at his typewriter, working on his new Venus story, when two sharp knocks at the bungalow door drew his attention away from the gargantuan beasts threatening his spaceman. He rose from the typing stand—wearing a white sportshirt, white slacks and tennis shoes (ready for his game with Hully)—and saw a familiar face through the screen door.

"I know you're a teetotaler now," Adam Sterling said, holding up frosty bottles of soda pop, "but I'm assuming that doesn't include root beer."

A broad-shouldered six-foot two, his brown hair graying at the temples, strong-jawed, deep-tanned Sterling might have been a hero out of one of Burroughs's own books—in fact, he looked a little like Herman Brix, that poor bastard who almost died playing Tarzan in the Guatemalan jungle for Florence's ex-husband.

"I can use something wet right now," Burroughs said through the screen. "You want to sit outside and chug those things?"

Sterling wore a white linen suit and a light blue tie; he'd apparently come from his office in the Dillingham Building in downtown Honolulu.

"No, Ed," he said, and he was almost whispering, "I'd like you to ask me in."

"Well come on in, then," Burroughs said, opening the door. "But it's stuffy as hell in here."

Stepping inside, Sterling said quietly, "Actually, Ed, I need to talk to you—in private. This isn't even for Hully's ears—he isn't around, is he?"

"No, he went down to the beach for a swim. Probably looking for his next girlfriend."

Sterling nodded, but—oddly—he took a quick walk around the one-bedroom bungalow, making sure he and the writer were indeed alone. Burroughs watched this not knowing whether to be amused or insulted.

Finally, they sat on the couch and sipped their root beers and Burroughs wondered what the hell was on the FBI man's mind.

"How goes the writing?" Sterling asked him.

He grunted. "Sometimes I think plots are like eggs."

"How so?"

"A hen's born able to lay just so many eggs, and after she's dropped her last one, she can sit on her nest and strain and grunt and never squeeze out another. I'm starting to think a writer is born with just so many plots."

A smile creased Sterling's face. "Why, have you been straining and grunting?"

"Hell, yes, and rearranging my feathers; but I'll be

damned if I can squeeze out a new plot, and these old ones are starting to smell."

Sterling shrugged. "I thought that last Tarzan, the one about the secret treasure, was swell."

"That was a movie, Adam—I didn't write that."

"Oh. Sorry."

"It did stink, though."

The FBI man took a swig of root beer. "You going to the luau tonight?"

"Those damn things . . . They expect you to eat dried octopus and raw fish and disinterred pig, and then there's that library paste they try to disguise under the alias of *poi*."

"Yeah, but are you going?"

"Haven't turned down an invite yet." Burroughs looked sideways at his friend, eyes slitted and amused. "Christ, Adam, I thought I was the worst conversationalist on the planet, till I heard this sorry attempt on your part. Can the small talk—what's this about?"

Sterling sighed, sat forward, hunkering toward him. "Ed, I need to take you into my confidence."

"Be my guest."

"This is very unofficial."

"Okay."

"I've been here at the Niumalu for about three months, now. So has somebody else."

Burroughs thought about that, gestured with a motion of his head. "That German next door, the big spender—Otto Kuhn. He and his wife moved in maybe a week before you."

"That's right. He's why I moved in, Ed."

"Really!" Burroughs got up from the couch, pulled his typing chair over and sat, so he could face his friend; this was getting interesting. "Don't tell me we have a Nazi at the Niumalu."

"Something like that. He's really just a goddamned beachcomber pretending to be a retired gentleman of substance. But . . . he *was* an officer in the Kaiser's Navy during the Great War, that much we know."

Burroughs arched an eyebrow. "He's trying to start a real estate business, I understand."

"That's just talk—before that it was selling furniture; for a while he studied Japanese at the University of Hawaii."

Now the writer was leaning forward. "Why does a German in English-speaking Hawaii want to learn Japanese?"

"Our boy Otto has frequent dealings with the Japs—he took one trip to Tokyo in '30 and another in '36. We suspect he's in their employ. My contacts confirm as much."

"Your contacts."

"Ed, you put our friend Colonel Frank Teske on his steamer today. I don't have to tell you he thinks war is imminent . . . that this island will be under attack, momentarily."

"What do you think, Adam?"

"He's right and he's wrong—war *is* imminent. Washington isn't having any luck negotiating with the Japanese. But Frank's wrong, too—the threat on our remote little island is not from the sky, but on the ground."

"Sabotage. I was just telling Hully the very same thing."

"Well, you're right. Since the middle of last year, I've been developing a network of contacts in the Japanese community—trustworthy ones, Americans who happen to be Japanese."

Both of the writer's eyebrows lifted. "Is there such a thing?"

"Oh yes. The vast majority of these Hawaii-born Japanese are loyal to our flag. And a number of them have been helping me identify the potentially dangerous sorts among them."

"What does that have to do with a German like Kuhn?"

Sterling spoke softly, but with an edge. "When the war begins, we'll be cracking down on disloyal Japs— arrests will be made. My contacts tell me that Kuhn is a 'sleeper' agent—set to take over as top local spy, when and if the top Japanese agents on this island are arrested, after hostilities begin."

"Your contacts are trustworthy? I mean, can you really trust these *nisei*?"

"I trust them," Sterling said. "But I also trust my fellow FBI agents, who've been keeping their eyes peeled. A little over a month ago, the *Tatsuta Maru* arrived in Honolulu, delivering a pair of Japanese diplomats, both of whom met with Kuhn—who then deposited fourteen thousand dollars in cash in a local bank."

Burroughs took another swig of the root beer.

"You've convinced me—he's a rat. Where do I come in?"

Sterling's face was a tight mask. "Things are heating up. This war *is* coming. I can use another pair of eyes here at the Niumalu . . . informed eyes . . . not to do any spying or poking around, understand—just to keep watch. I'm not here during the day, and Kuhn frequently is."

"You're not asking me to do surveillance—take notes . . ."

"No. Just keep your head up. Stay alert. Let me know if you see anything, anyone, suspicious around Kuhn or his cottage."

"Glad to help," Burroughs said.

"All right, then—mum's the word." Sterling slapped his thighs, and rose. "See you tonight at the luau?"

Burroughs stood. "I'll be there—just don't pass me any of that goddamn library paste."

The FBI man chuckled, shook the writer's hand, collected the empty soda-pop bottles, and went out, leaving an energized Burroughs behind.

Feeling revitalized, Edgar Rice Burroughs returned to Venus, wondering if this time he might make it to the fire before it went out.

# THREE

## *Luau Luminaries*

The Niumalu was noted for its luaus, which were held once a month. Guests often asked why the hotel didn't hold their version of a native feast every week, but the truth was, it took seven to ten days to properly prepare for the event.

The central set piece of the affair was itself a day-long chore: the roasting of a kalua pig, hoofs and all. The pig was stuffed with hot rocks, lowered into a barbecue pit called an *imu,* which was already filled with red-hot rocks, then the unprotesting pig was covered with *ti* leaves, buried under earth and canvas, and left to slowly cook, hour upon hour.

The result was melt-in-your-mouth succulence, a tender, delicious, fall-off-the-bone meat the likes of which Hully Burroughs had never tasted. Hully was an ardent supporter of the picturesque ritual—even if O. B. did dismiss the tradition of roasting a pig in an *imu* as "a lot of silly fuss over cooking some damn pork."

All day long, hotel manager Fred Bivens and his staff had been bustling around the palm-shaded grounds, in particular dealing with deliveries of food-stuffs. That little Japanese grocer, Yoshio Harada, had been bringing pickup-truckloads of fresh fish and pro-duce over from his shop at the Aala Market in Chi-natown. That afternoon, Hully—in his tennis whites, waiting to meet his father on the court—had helped the nice little guy unload for a while, making a few trips to the rear kitchen door.

Harada—slight, mustached, primly businesslike in a white short-sleeved shirt with a red tie—had an "in" with the hotel staff: his niece, Pearl, was the featured singer with the Niumalu band, which was a popular local attraction.

"You are very kind, Burroughs-*san*," Harada said. "Pearl speak very well of you."

"She's never given me the time of day, though," Hully said, hauling a bushel basket of sweet potatoes.

"Pearl is popular girl," the grocer said, smile flashing under the neatly trimmed mustache, the little man carrying enough bananas to send Tarzan's pet monkey into a frenzy.

Actually, Hully was aware that the pretty singer—who indeed had been "popular," dating any number of guys in recent months—was seriously seeing Ensign Bill Fielder, a good pal of Hully's. But he didn't men-tion this to the grocer, as he wasn't sure how the Jap-anese gent would react to his daughter dating a *haole*.

When Hully wandered over to the tennis court to wait for his dad, he discovered Pearl sunbathing on the strip of sand nearby. Hully and the singer were friendly, but (as he'd indicated to her uncle) she'd always been involved with one guy or another, and he never seemed to get his turn.

He would've loved to have one: she was a stunning girl in her early twenties, with black hair and a slender, curvy form made obvious by a formfitting pink bathing suit, petite at five-two or -three, with wonderful high cheekbones, a flawless complexion and full lips that always seemed poised to pucker into a kiss. Her father, back home in San Francisco, was Japanese; but her mother, also in Frisco, was white, and the Eurasian combination was exquisite. If he hadn't known of her Japanese blood, Hully would never have guessed its presence, her dark eyes lacking the distinctive Asian almond shape; still, something exotic lurked in those features.

Before his father showed up for tennis, Hully sat hugging his knees on the sand, next to Pearl, and they chatted. She was on her back, half sitting, leaning on her elbows.

"I suppose Bill's got your dance card filled tonight," he said.

Her smile was lazy yet dazzling and as white as her name. "I only get to dance on a few songs—I have to sing for my supper, you know. . . . Is Bill's father going to be here tonight?"

Colonel Kendall Fielder, chief of Army intelligence,

was a good friend of the elder Burroughs, and frequently stopped by the Niumalu.

"I think so," Hully said. "He's a regular at these luaus."

She seemed troubled. "I hope the colonel won't mind seeing his son dance with the likes of me."

"He'll only be jealous."

The smile returned. "If Bill's father breaks us up, how about catching me on the rebound?"

Hully felt his heart race—foolish though that was. "Why wait?"

She shrugged, stared toward the vast blue of the ocean, visible through an opening in the palms and across a stubby fence guarding a short drop-off. "I don't think your father would like me much, either. He always growls at me."

"He growls at everybody. Anyway, he doesn't think for me—I'm free, wuh . . ." He paused.

"White and twenty-one?" The smile was sad now, but no less lovely. "Don't kid yourself, Hully. These are . . . precarious times. You know Colonel Fielder well, don't you?"

"Fairly well. He and my pop are tight as ticks."

The lovely dark eyes tightened. "Do you think you . . . or your father . . . could introduce us? I'd really like to talk to Colonel Fielder."

"I'm sure you could meet him."

A strange sense of urgency throbbed in the girl's voice. "I really need to see him, alone. . . . Would you help me? Perhaps speak to your father, and ask him to arrange a meeting?"

"Well . . . sure."

Hully's heart wasn't racing now. The breathtaking Pearl simply wanted his help so she could make her case to her beau's father—which no doubt meant Bill had finally popped the question. And Hully felt sad for her, sorry for her, because he knew how the colonel was likely to respond, in this climate of war clouds, to the notion of his son marrying a *nisei*.

Then his father had arrived, and Hully hopped up from the sand and joined the old man on the court. The tantalizing aroma of the nearby roasting pig offered a distraction almost as bad as Pearl in her pink bathing suit, and Hully again lost to his old man, two sets to one.

As he and his dad headed back to the bungalow for cool showers—the Niumalu's accommodations lacked water heaters, typical here in this land of perfect temperatures—Hully told his father that he'd put them in for the luau.

They were moving past hedges of hibiscus and morning glory flowering beneath poinciana and jacaranda trees.

"I'd rather go to the wrestling match," O. B. grumbled, "and eat hot dogs."

Hully knew his dad wasn't kidding: they frequently attended the professional wrestling bouts at several local arenas, particularly when the champ, Prince Ali Hassan, was competing, as he was tonight; O. B. found the sport "hilariously exciting," relishing what he termed the "sweaty theatricality" and "hokey sadism."

"You know a lot of your Navy and Army pals will

be here," Hully said, opening the bungalow door for his dad. Nearby, orchids bloomed in coconut shells hanging from a monkey pod. "The brass always turns out for these Niumalu luaus."

"I'm sure there'll be the usual quota of admirals and colonels," O. B. said, stepping inside. "These admirals are so plentiful they get between your feet and in your hair. I have to comb 'em out every time I come home."

"What hair?" Hully asked, good-naturedly. "Anyway, you love those Navy guys."

"Compared to the Army brass, sure," the old boy said, flopping on the couch. "Our Navy is great, but that Army of ours is undermanned and underequipped, if you ask me."

"I don't remember asking, Pop," Hully said, sitting next to him. "Anyway, Fred said for us, the luau's on the house, as usual."

"Because I'm a celebrity. You know notoriety gives me a royal pain."

Hully also knew his father had once loved publicity—it was the adverse publicity surrounding the Burroughs divorce and remarriage that led to this new-found phobia.

"Anyway, I'm unquestionably the world's poorest conversationalist," O. B. said, folding his arms. "I'm as bad a listener as these idiots are lousy talkers—average man or woman has little or nothing worth saying, and spend much of their waking lives saying it. They exercise their vocal organs while their brains atrophy."

Hully was used to such rants. Calmly he said, "I'm not going to the wrestling match, Pop. Anyway, you're a great conversationalist, and some very interesting people are bound to be there. You're just not used to socializing sober."

Burroughs gave his son a blank, almost stunned look; then the old man burst into laughter.

"You got me," he said. "Take your damn shower—you smell worse than I do."

Hully took his shower.

He was amused by his father's cantankerousness, and delighted by how the old man's despondency had faded over the last month or so. Frankly amazed by his father's new lease on life, Hully had marveled the other day when, walking back to the hotel along a fence line, his father had jumped up, swung a leg over and dropped down nimbly on the other side. The younger Burroughs had stood there flabbergasted: the fence was chest-high, and Hully knew *he* couldn't have vaulted the thing.

Perhaps it was time to get back home, to his mother, in the house in Bel Air. He was well aware she suffered from chronic alcoholism—he'd witnessed her incessant drinking since his childhood. Her periods of sobriety were now very short—a week or two—followed by ten days to two weeks of a bender resulting in delirium tremens and, ultimately, a doctor's care. Hully knew the affliction would follow his mother to the grave—if it didn't send her there, first.

Nothing remained but to try to make her life as happy and as free of worry as possible, and to keep her from injuring herself. Shortly before he left, he'd fired a maid and driver who were aiding and abetting his mother's bingeing, and taking advantage of her financially.

Truth was, he was enjoying himself here in Hawaii, and dreaded going back home—he loved spending time with his father, adored Waikiki with its gentle, flower-scented breezes, and had enjoyed several brief romances here . . . even if Pearl Harada hadn't been one of them.

A hundred guests had descended upon the Niumalu by sundown, far more than the relatively few residents of the thirty cottages scattered about the tropical grounds. The tables in the dining room had been rearranged, fit together picnic-style, but Hully and his father—and another forty patrons, inclined toward a more authentic, traditional presentation—sat like Indians on the lawn on lau hala mats, gathered around a long narrow spread of food exhibiting great variety and color, including the exotic likes of *lomi-lomi* (salmon rubbed and raw, mixed with shaved ice, onions and tomatoes); *ti*-wrapped breadfruit, yams, bananas and beef; *opii* (raw limpets); *pipikaula* (Hawaiian jerked beef); *limu* (dried seaweed); *laulau,* parcels of pork with salted butterfish; and two kinds of *poi,* one made from breadfruit, the other of *taro*. And chicken and mahimahi and, of course, the delicious shredded pork from the *imu*. Eventually *noupio* (coconut pudding) was served, but it took a long while, and a lot of serious eating, to get there. . . .

Hully and his father both capitulated to having wine with their meals, passing on the stronger stuff—*oke,* short for *okolehao,* ginlike booze derived from *ti* root and, according to O. B., "every bit as good as horse liniment." Free-flowing *oke* and wine made the evening even more festive, and casual, and it was plenty casual, with even some of the admirals and colonels wearing the currently popular, colorful silk "aloha" shirts, the women in loose-fitting, equally colorful muumuus, or the occasional kimono—Japanese fashion and culture were much admired locally, despite the threat of war.

In fact, the top brass themselves were here tonight— Admiral Husband E. Kimmel, commander of the Pacific Fleet, and Lieutenant General Walter C. Short, commander of the U.S. Army ground and air forces. Kimmel wore a white suit with a light gray tie that vaguely invoked his Naval dress whites, while Short was in a red-and-yellow aloha shirt.

Hully's father knew both men. Kimmel and Short sat almost directly across from O. B.—the two most powerful military men on the island had arrived together, with petite, attractive Mrs. Short (it was well-known that Kimmel had left his wife on the mainland, so as not to be distracted in his Hawaiian duty . . . even if his name was Husband).

As usual, Kimmel—whose strong voice was touched with a Kentucky bluegrass twang—seemed uncomfortable in a casual setting, his broad brow troubled. The admiral was in his late fifties, five feet ten inches of compact muscle and bone, his dark blond hair graying at the temples, with clear, direct blue eyes, a slightly hooked nose, and a sternly set mouth and chin.

Short, on the other hand, was affable and easygoing,

and the close friendship between the admiral and the general puzzled many, as they would seem personal and professional opposites. A slim, wiry five feet ten, in his early sixties, Short had a thin, delicately boned, sensitive face with deep-set eyes under frequently lifted brows, with a high-bridged nose and a thin upper lip and sensuous lower one.

"Ed," Short was saying, helping himself to two fingers of *poi* (no utensils allowed at a luau), "how did a fellow with a military background like you wind up an *artiste*?"

"Nobody's ever accused me of being an artist before, General," Burroughs said, nibbling a chunk of banana. "Biggest disappointment of my life was when Teddy Roosevelt turned me down for the Rough Riders."

Short frowned and smiled simultaneously. "I thought you were in the cavalry—the 'Bloody Seventh,' who fought at Little Bighorn and Wounded Knee."

"That's true, but the press agents would have you believe I fought side by side with Custer."

"Maybe that's what happened to your scalp," Hully kidded.

His father laughed at that, continuing, "The only Indians I came in contact with, at Fort Grant, were Indian scouts. No, my cavalry career was undistinguished, General. A flop like everything else I ever tried."

"Edgar Rice Burroughs," Kimmel said, putting some pomp into the name, "a flop? That seems unlikely."

"Admiral, I have sold electric lightbulbs to janitors, candy to drugstores and peddled Stoddard's lectures door-to-door. The only interesting job I ever had was as a policeman."

This was news to Hully, sitting next to his father. "You were a cop, Pop?"

Burroughs smiled at the admiral and general, pointing a thumb at his son. "You see, my boy has inherited my literary skill." Then he turned to Hully. "Yes, my poetic offspring, I was a police officer in Salt Lake City, my principal duty rousting drunks and hoboes. Even flashed my gun a few times."

Hully was impressed. "When was this?"

"Maybe ought three, ought four . . . don't really remember, exactly. But mostly I was a salesman—a bad one. I was peddling pencil sharpeners when I first took up writing."

"Had you always had an interest in literature?" Kimmel asked.

"I liked Mark Twain, and *The Prisoner of Zenda,* if you call that literature. I was supervising other salesmen, had a lot of free time, and spent it reading cheap magazines. The fiction I read struck me as lousy, and I figured if other people could get paid for writing such rotten stuff, make room for Burroughs."

"I like your books, Ed," Short said, grinning, "and I won't have you downgrading yourself . . . and my good taste."

"Don't think I'm not grateful, General. No writer alive has taken more potshots than me—there are librarians and literary types who consider my stuff a bad influence, particularly on young minds like yours."

The general laughed, and said, "How on earth could Tarzan be considered harmful?"

"Well, a good number of kids have fallen out of trees, emulating him . . . otherwise, I think it's good for their imaginations."

Mrs. Short said, rather primly, "Don't you think some children have rather overactive imaginations, Mr. Burroughs?"

"With all due respect, Mrs. Short, the power of imagination is all that differentiates the human from the brute. Without imagination, there's no power to visualize what we have never experienced . . . and without that, there can be no progress, no invention."

Hully smiled to himself, thinking of his father's self-characterization of being a "lousy conversationalist." Of course, giving in to a little wine had lubricated his dad's tongue, no question. . . .

Kimmel was frowning in thought. "How on earth did you come up with something as imaginative as Tarzan?"

The half smirk disappeared from O. B.'s face and his response was surprisingly serious—in fact, Hully would never forget what his father quietly, humbly said next.

"Frankly, Admiral, I suppose it came out of my daily life consisting of such drab, dull business matters. I think I just wanted to get as far away from commerce as possible—so my mind roamed in scenes and situations I never knew." He gestured to the tropical trees around them. "I've never been to Africa, you know—

but I find I can write better about places I've never seen than those I have."

"Excuse me, Mr. Burroughs," said the young Japanese man seated on O. B.'s other side, "but I wonder if you are aware of how very popular you are in my country?"

This was Tadashi Morimura, who had introduced himself earlier—a diplomat in his late twenties, vice consul of the Japanese Consulate in Honolulu. Like Kimmel, Morimura wore a white suit and a tie; he was a boyish, slender man, his longish black hair brushed back on a smooth, high forehead.

"Well, I've had good foreign sales for years, though this European war is playing havoc with 'em."

"My cousin is named Edgar," Morimura said, with a shy smile. "Sir, I know many boys who have been named for you."

O. B. seemed genuinely touched. "That's the first I've heard of that. But I don't see why a boy in your country wouldn't respond to what kids here do—kids including General Short, of course."

"You mean the constant urge for escape," Kimmel said thoughtfully, even a little pompously. "To trade the confines of city streets for the freedom of the wilderness . . ."

"I think it's more," O. B. said. "I think on some primal level, we all would like to throw off the restrictions of man-made laws, the inhibitions that society has placed on us. Every boy, of any age, would like to be Tarzan . . . I know I would."

"As would I," Morimura said, raising his cup of wine.

Despite the pleasantness of the evening, the great food, the wonderful conversation, Hully couldn't help but be struck by the surreal incongruity of this social gathering: the commanders of the Army and Navy sharing *poi* with a Japanese diplomat, when everyone seemed to agree war between their two countries was both inevitable and imminent.

But Morimura seemed a pleasant sort, harmless, well-spoken, typically polite.

As the dining wound down, the entertainment increased, the evening alive with flaming torches and swinging swords, and various renditions of the hula from seductive, lyrical swaying to the frenetic hip-twitching version tourists craved. Wandering troubadours with ukuleles and steel guitars sang traditional Hawaiian standards, but also Tin Pan Alley island fare like "Sweet Leilani" and "Blue Hawaii."

By around ten, the luau proper was over and the guests were milling around the grounds, lounging throughout the lodge, in the rock-garden courtyard, and in the enclosed rear *lanai,* with its wicker furnishings and soothing view onto a tropical garden. The music, however, had shifted to the big-band music of Pearl and the Harbor Lights on the dance floor adjacent to the dining room.

Hully and his father split up—he noticed O. B. talking to Colonel Fielder at one point, out on the lawn, and to that German playboy Otto Kuhn, in the rock garden—and the younger Burroughs sat at a table with

Ensign Bill Fielder and Seaman Dan Pressman, smoking cigarettes, drinking *oke* (except for Hully, who had switched from wine to coffee), listening to Pearl and the band do "Oh, Look at Me Now."

The only concession to Hawaiian-style music made by Pearl and the Harbor Lights was the inclusion of two guitars, one of them steel, and of course the boys in the band did wear blue aloha shirts with a yellow-and-red floral pattern. Bathed in pale pink stage lighting, Pearl—standing at her center-stage microphone, which she occasionally touched, in a sensually caressing fashion—wore a clinging blue gown, with a daring décolletage that showed off her medium-size but firm, high breasts to fine advantage.

"I'm going to tell the old man tonight," Bill was saying. He was a handsome Naval officer in his early twenties with dark hair and a cleft chin—despite his crisply military haircut, he looked more like a kid than a sailor, in his green aloha shirt and white slacks.

"I can see what you see in Pearl," Hully said, and he certainly could, his eyes returning to the ethereal, erotic vision she made on stage under the pink lighting in the low-cut blue gown. "But you've only been going with her for a month. . . . Can't you wait—"

"What, till war breaks out, and I'm at sea, fighting her relatives?" Bill's dark eyes were sharp, but his speech was slightly slurred—too much *oke*. "There's not going to be a better time to break this to Dad—certainly after we're at war with Japan, it's not gonna be any easier."

"Bill," his friend Dan said, a blue-eyed blond sailor

from California, "she's a nice girl, and I mean you'd have to be blind not to see she's a living doll . . . but you gotta admit—she's been around."

"Take that back!" Bill said, stiffening.

"Okay, okay," Dan said, patting the air with his palms. "I didn't mean she was . . . fast or anything. Just that she's dated a few guys. . . . Maybe you should wait a couple months, get to know each other better."

"Dan's right," Hully said. "Wait a little bit—get past the physical attraction and know each other as people . . . just to make sure. . . ."

"I *am* sure—Pearl's the girl for me. She's sweet and she's nice and she'll give everything up for me, her singing, everything . . . just to be my wife and have my babies."

"Maybe you ought to think about that, too," Dan said.

Bill glared at him. "What?"

"What it'll put your kids through—you know, the racial thing."

"Pearl's half white. Our kids'll be all American. Dan, I won't hear this kind of talk."

"Okay, buddy . . . I'm just trying to help. You've helped me before, plenty of times—I'm just trying to be your friend."

Bill sighed and nodded.

The band was starting to play "I'll Remember April," and one of the guitar players began to sing the lilting ballad. Bill shot out of his chair as if from a cannon, muttering, "This is one of Pearl's free songs," and headed for the bandstand.

Then he was out there dancing with her, holding her close, gazing into her eyes like a lovesick puppy, and she was gazing back, a beautiful woman who seemed equally in love. It was romantic, and frightening.

"His father is going to kick Bill's ass," Dan said.

"I know," Hully said, and nodded toward the entry-way to the lobby.

Colonel Fielder—slim, casually attired in red aloha shirt and white slacks, his dark hair widow's-peaked, with a narrow face and hawkish eyes and hawkish nose—stood just inside the doorway, staring out at the dance floor, obviously viewing his son dancing with the *nisei* singer—and just as obviously unhappy.

Shaking his head in apparent disgust, Fielder exited.

"It's gonna be ugly," Dan said.

"Pearl asked me to set up a meeting between her and the colonel—she wants to plead her case."

"If she thinks batting her lashes at that hardnose is going to do the trick, she's dreamin'."

Out on the dance floor, something "ugly" was already transpiring. A soldier—a handsome brown-haired kid in a green sportshirt and tan slacks, not very tall but with wide shoulders and an athletic carriage—was tapping Bill on the shoulder—hard—as if to cut in.

"Oh hell," Hully said, shaking his head.

"Who is that guy?" Dan asked.

"Jack Stanton—he's a corporal over at Hickam . . . used to date Pearl."

"Ouch."

"Fact, that's who she threw over for Bill."

"Double ouch."

Out on the dance floor, Pearl was desperately trying to keep the peace as the sailor and the soldier began shoving each other.

"You take Bill," Hully said, getting up, "I got the dogface."

The crowd was forming a circle around what was clearly about to erupt into a fight, with reactions that ranged from shouts of indignation to squeals of delight. Hully and Dan broke through just in time to see Stanton connect with a right hook to Bill's jaw.

Bill went down on a knee, but came up with his own right hand to the soldier's belly, doubling the boy over.

And the fight was over before Hully and Dan could break it up, because the soldier—like everyone here— had been to that sumptuous, endless luau, and his stomach . . . filled with *poi* and raw fish and roast pork and a dozen other delicacies . . . did not take a punch well.

The soldier, clutching his stomach, scrambled out of there, struggling not to throw up, heading for the men's room, as relieved laughter rippled across the crowd. Soon the onlookers began to dance again, the Harbor Lights beginning to play "Boogie Woogie Bugle Boy," with Pearl magically back onstage to sing it.

"I'm going after that bastard," Bill said, lurching forward, and Hully grabbed him around the arms, from behind.

Hully whispered harshly in his friend's ear. "You get back to the *Arizona*—you want your dad to see this? Much less get wind of what this fight is about?"

Bill, *oke* or not, sighed and nodded.

"Get him the hell out of here," Hully said to Dan.

"Sure thing," Dan said, and took charge of his friend, walking him out.

Then, suddenly, O. B. was at Hully's side. "Did I miss some action?"

"Just a sailor and a soldier, fighting over a dame," Hully said.

Jitterbuggers were jumping and kicking before them.

O. B. asked, over the blaring music, "Fielder's son?"

Hully nodded.

The old man shook his head, nodded up toward the pretty girl in the low-cut blue dress, her breasts jiggling provocatively as she sang the up-tempo tune.

"That little Pearl of the Pacific up there," he said, "is gonna get some poor fool killed."

And then O. B. turned and went out, leaving his son to marvel at how little got past his old man.

# FOUR

# Nightmare at the Beach

At the luau, after his son had gone in to enjoy the dance band, Burroughs sought out his friend Colonel Kendall "Wooch" Fielder, and chatted on the Niumalu lawn under the soft pastel glow of Japanese lanterns . . . an irony lost on neither man.

Burroughs sipped a glass of red wine, and the slim, hawkish-countenanced Fielder worked on both a cocktail and a cigarette. Wooch—a nickname that dated to the colonel's Georgia Tech football days—was a frequent participant in Niumalu poker games. Sunday through Thursday, curfew requirements kept everyone but officials indoors, and card games had become a favorite pastime.

Lots of drinking went on at these "whiskey poker" games, and Burroughs had kept active, despite his current abstinence from the hard stuff. He loved poker with a passion, and was accepted as "boss of the play and ruler on all technicalities."

Fielder was a key player because liquor was rationed, but as a high-ranking officer, Wooch could bring unallotted bottles from the officers' club.

"Listen, Wooch," Burroughs said, "I want a correspondent's card. With war coming, no one's gonna give a damn about fiction writing—I want to get in the thick of it, and write about what's really going on."

"Ed," Fielder said, smiling, exhaling smoke, "what the hell do you want to fool with that nonsense for? A man of your reputation, a man your age . . ."

"An old fart, you mean. A hundred bucks says I can do more sit-ups than you—right here, right now."

Fielder laughed, a little. "And here I always thought you talked that way because you were drinking."

"Well, I *have* had a little wine—but come on, Wooch . . . you can hook me up, you can wrangle me that card. I want to see some action."

"Let's wait till there's some action to see, why don't we?"

Over to their left, in the flicker of torchlight, standing near one of the bungalows which was draped in purple and rose-colored bougainvillea, General Short was engaged in a smiling conversation with Morimura of the Japanese Consulate. Mrs. Short, in a floral muumuu, was at the general's side, and a pretty Oriental girl, with contemporary makeup and hairstyle but wearing a kimono, was on Morimura's arm. Everyone had cocktails in hand.

"What's the story on the toothy little Jap diplomat?" Burroughs asked Fielder.

"If that pipsqueak is all Tojo has in store for us,"

Fielder said, snorting a laugh, "we don't have much to worry about. Intelligence clears him—inexperienced, doesn't show up on any list of attachés."

"Why is the brass so friendly with him?"

"What's the harm? Morimura spends most of his days playing golf, and his nights in nightclubs and restaurants. He drinks heavily, and I understand practically lives at the Shuncho-ro."

That was a well-known teahouse on Alawa Heights overlooking Honolulu.

"Well, hell, Wooch—that would give the little bastard a ringside view of Pearl Harbor, and Hickam Field to boot."

"The only view that amiable buffoon is interested in is the teahouse girls, like that one he escorted here, tonight. He's taken half the geishas in Honolulu on glass-bottom boat rides around Pearl Harbor."

"Sounds to me like he makes a habit out of socializing around battleships."

Fielder gestured with his cocktail in hand, sighed smoke. "Ed, a certain amount of espionage is to be expected. How can we keep the Japanese consulate from studying local newspapers, and listening to local radio broadcasts? . . . As for the ships in Pearl Harbor, all a 'spy' has to do is perch someplace and watch. It's legal—we do the same damn thing to them."

Arching an eyebrow, Burroughs said, "You'll notice that smiling, sociable Mr. Morimura keeps his distance from our German friend, Mr. Kuhn."

"Your point being, what? That they're in league, helping each other spy? Those playboy clowns?"

The writer shook his head. "You don't read enough pulp fiction, Wooch—ever hear of the Scarlet Pimpernel, or Zorro?"

"Kuhn and Morimura are harmless fools—not that I don't agree with you, Ed, that all this . . . fraternization . . . is unsettling."

And with that statement, Wooch Fielder's expression shifted, or had Burroughs simply not noticed the anxiety in the man's narrow eyes?

The colonel moved near Burroughs, his manner more intimate, his tone a near whisper. "Ed, your son and my son are close . . . as close as we are."

"I'd say so."

"Would you ask Hully if he's heard anything about Bill and that . . . that little Japanese singer?"

Burroughs, who knew damn well Bill Fielder had been dating Pearl Harada, said only, "Be glad to check."

"This morning, I had an anonymous call to that effect. . . . I don't usually pay much heed to such things, but . . . Christ, Ed, you don't think Bill could be that foolish, do you?"

With General Short visible in laughing conversation with the Japanese vice consul, Burroughs said, "Wooch, she's a pretty girl. If you were young and healthy, would you think about politics, or that Hedy Lamarr face and figure?"

Fielder drew on the cigarette, nodded, dropped the spent butt to the grass and heeled it out. "I think I'll peek in there and see for myself. Bill and his pals are in listening to her band—maybe it's time for me to do a little espionage work of my own."

Burroughs put a hand on his friend's shoulder. "Don't be hard on the boy, Wooch. You were young once. Hell, even I was."

Fielder nodded, barely, and strode toward the Niumalu lodge, from which emanated the muffled sound of the band playing "I'll Remember April."

Burroughs, cup of wine in hand, wandered, stopping now and then for conversation. A few guests were chatting in the hotel courtyard—not a spacious area, particularly since the hub was taken up by a rock-garden, and standing room was compromised by the yawning fronds of potted tropical plants on the periphery. The dining room was open onto this rock-garden courtyard, and the loud, lively dance music of Pearl and her Harbor Lights limited conversation, as well.

But Burroughs was amused to find Otto Kuhn—his blonde wife on his arm, "playboy" or not—chatting with secret adversary Adam Sterling of the FBI.

Kuhn—even at six foot, still towered over by the strapping, brown-haired FBI agent—had blue-eyed bland good looks, dark blond hair and wore a white linen suit with a silver tie. Elfriede Kuhn was of medium height, with a nicely slender shape, and one of the few women present not swimming in a muumuu or wrapped up in a kimono—she wore a simple black cocktail dress, rather low-cut. Both husband and wife were attractive individuals in their dissipated forties.

The conversation was focused on an upcoming battle: the annual Shrine-sponsored football game tomorrow, in which the University of Hawaii would meet Willamette. The German favored Hawaii, while the FBI agent—a Willamette University graduate, it happened—not unexpectedly argued for the out-of-town team.

Burroughs, who didn't give a damn either way—he was a boxing and wrestling fan—stood on the fringes of the conversation, politely; then the German—his blue eyes languid—changed the subject, drawing Burroughs directly in.

"I feel my countrymen owe you an apology, Edgar," Kuhn said, his accent thick, his manner smooth. "It is something I have long meant to bring up."

"Why an apology?" Burroughs asked, already amused.

"Like so many German men, when was it . . . ten years ago? I was a devoted fan of your Tarzan novels. What a sensation you were in my homeland!"

Burroughs sipped his wine, offered up a wry smile. "That is true—my first German royalty check was the largest single foreign payment I ever had."

"Every man and boy in Deutschland caught Tarzan fever," Kuhn said, admiringly, eyes as bright as any young fan of the Jungle Lord's adventures.

Mildly chagrined, the writer said, "Well, like most epidemics, it ran its course. Or I should say, got cured."

"What was done to you was most unfortunate," the German said, shaking his head, "most unfair."

Her pretty features pinched with sympathy, Kuhn's wife said, "Oh, yes, how foolishly the press behaved."

The FBI agent, confused, said, "What was done to you, Ed?"

"Well, it was my own damn fault, or my agent's— after we did so well with the first four Tarzans, a rival publisher bought the rights to a book my regular German publisher had skipped over—*Tarzan the Untamed,* a thing I did during the world war."

Eyebrow arched, Kuhn glanced at Sterling. "It was published as *Tarzan der Deutschenfresser.* . . . It too caused a sensation."

Sterling still appeared confused, and Mrs. Kuhn further translated, her manner as delicate as her words were not: *"Tarzan the German Devourer."*

Now the FBI man got it—perhaps, as the Tarzan fan he had often professed to be, he even recalled the plot of the novel: Tarzan—his beloved wife Jane apparently murdered by a German officer—goes on a blood-lust rampage against the Hun, including setting loose a ravenous lion in the German trenches.

"You can't give my stuff away there, now," Burroughs said, with a laugh. "As Mrs. Kuhn said, the German press lambasted me—one article advised readers to throw their Tarzan books into the garbage can."

"Sanctimonious nonsense," the German said. "Were you expected to soft-pedal your honest convictions, at the height of a bitter war?"

"Well, I should have seen it coming, and blocked publication in Germany—it was dated material, wartime propaganda, and shouldn't have been reprinted, anywhere."

Sterling said, "I guess politics and entertainment

don't mix. You've never regained your footing over there, in all this time?"

Kuhn answered for Burroughs, "Adam, you don't realize the extent of our friend's popularity—the fever turned into a furor. . . ."

Sterling frowned. "What does Hitler have to do with it?"

Burroughs laughed, almost choking on his wine. "Not 'führer,' Adam—fur-or."

Embarrassed, the FBI man said, "Sorry."

"An understandable confusion," the German said urbanely. "After all, there *were* public burnings of your books, Edgar."

Mrs. Kuhn asked the writer, "Did your German publishers ever ask you to offer an . . . explanation, or apology to your readers?"

"An open letter from me was published," Burroughs said, and Kuhn—aware of this—was nodding. "I didn't apologize, exactly. The novel reflected what I thought and felt at the time I wrote it. I wasn't about to assume a spineless attitude and retract and apologize ad nauseam."

With a nod—though stopping short of clicking his heels—Kuhn said, "Well, please allow me to offer an overdue apology myself, on behalf of the German people."

"Thanks, Otto—though I prefer royalties to apologies."

But much later that evening, after the last luau guests had departed the Niumalu, Burroughs—in his bungalow, preparing for bed—reflected on *Tarzan the Un-*

*tamed,* which since the German uproar had been withheld from all markets. The businessman in him was thinking that the book was probably marketable again—and, when the war came, could go back into print, in America anyway. Tarzan bellowing the victory cry of the bull ape as he stood with his foot on the chest of a fallen German soldier, whose neck he'd snapped . . . that could prove to be a crowd-pleaser again, before too very long. . . .

Though it was after midnight, Hully wasn't home yet—off having a good time with his sailor pals, no doubt, prowling Hotel Street. Burroughs was in his pajama bottoms—he liked to sleep shirtless, in this tropical clime—about to shut off the light and climb in bed when a knock at the door interrupted him. Grumbling, he threw on a maroon rayon robe and went to the door.

"Could I come in for a moment?" Pearl Harada asked, looking up at him through the screen door. The dark eyes in the lovely face conveyed urgency, and she seemed small, childlike, gazing up from the bottom step of the stoop.

"If you're looking for Hully . . ."

"No, Mr. Burroughs—it's you I want to see." She was still wearing the low-cut gown, but a lacy shawl was slung around her shoulders, and over her décolletage, whether out of modesty, or because of the cool night breeze, Burroughs couldn't say.

He opened the screen door, glanced around, wondering if allowing this young beauty into his bungalow was an impropriety he'd pay for; then he sighed and nodded, gesturing her inside.

He suggested she sit on the couch, which she did, and offered her a soft drink, which she refused.

"I won't be here long," she assured him. "I know it's late . . . and I know this is an imposition. But it really is important."

"All right," he said, pulling his typing chair over, sitting opposite her.

"Has your son spoken to you about me?"

"No he hasn't."

Her eyes lowered to her lap, where her hands were clasped. "Hully's a nice boy—he probably will say something. But I saw him leave with Bill . . . and I couldn't take the chance."

"What chance?"

"That he would forget to ask you."

"Ask me what?"

"If . . . if you would arrange a meeting for me, with Bill's father."

"Oh, my. . . . Young lady, please don't put me in the middle of—"

She sat forward, her eyes glittering, the shawl slipping, and he did his best not to look down into the considerable cleavage of this girl who was young enough to be his daughter. "Oh, Mr. Burroughs, I know you're a good man, a considerate man, underneath that . . . gruff exterior."

"Underneath this gruff exterior, my dear, is a gruff interior."

"I don't believe it—I can see kindness in your eyes. I know Colonel Fielder doesn't approve of us, Bill and I. . . ."

"Can you blame him, at a time like this?"

She shook her head, and the dark arcs of hair swung. "That's why I have to speak with the colonel—I have to speak with him privately, and I know you can arrange that. Discreetly, Mr. Burroughs. It's important."

"You want a private meeting with Colonel Fielder. Just you and him—not Bill."

She was nodding. "I need to state my own case. I want to prove myself to Bill's father."

Burroughs smiled, shook his head. "You're a determined young woman."

"Yes I am."

He couldn't help it: she impressed him. She was as intelligent as she was beautiful, and she had courage and conviction. Who could blame any man for loving a woman like this?

"I've written about women like you," he told her. "But I've met damn few."

"I . . . I don't understand."

He stood, holding out his hand to her. "I'll help you. I'll talk to Colonel Fielder, and set the meeting up here at my bungalow . . . discreetly. Tomorrow soon enough?"

"Oh, Mr. Burroughs," she said, beaming, and she almost threw herself off the couch into his arms, holding on to him, tight. Face pressed sideways against his chest, she said, "Hully is a lucky boy, having a father like you."

"Yeah, I'm a peach." He patted her back, gently. "Now get out of here before I fall in love with you, myself, you little vixen. Scoot!"

The dark eyes were teary with joy, her smile a white slash of happiness, as she scurried out of the bungalow, thanking him as she went.

Wishing he were thirty years younger, Burroughs sighed and headed into the bedroom. *There's a Jane any Tarzan might fall for,* he thought. He slipped out of the robe and—bare-chested, in the pajama bottoms—crawled under a single sheet of his bed, a flower-scented breeze whispering in the open window, fluffing sheer curtains, the lap of waves on the nearby beach soothing him, lulling him to sleep.

Deep asleep, dreaming, he believed he'd awakened, hearing a sound. In his dream, he opened eyes that in reality were tightly shut, and saw—shrouded in darkness—a figure standing across the room from him. The figure gradually revealed itself to be female—a tall, beautiful female who moved into a shaft of pure, heavenly light, slanting through the window.

The woman's flesh was an emerald green, her hair scarlet, her voluptuous body bare but for strategic scatterings of gold sequins that appeared to have been applied to her naked skin. She seemed to be approaching him, reaching out to him, and he sat up, and reached out for her. . . .

A roar from the darkness—for the bedroom had become a cave—announced a third player, and a mammoth man-beast lumbered into view . . . a pair of tusks, a huge single eye, a fiercely muscular build matted with fur with two arms on either side, each thick pawlike hand clutching a scimitarlike blade, four swords slashing at the air, threatening the green woman, who fell as the blades cleaved her emerald flesh, blood the color of gold splashing, and Burroughs tried to move, but found himself paralyzed in bed, screaming in protest, unable to move, too late to save the beautiful emerald girl, too late. . . .

Then he was sitting up in bed, drenched in sweat, catching himself in mid-scream.

Quickly Burroughs got up out of bed, raced to his typewriter, snapped on his desk lamp, and sat in front of the keyboard, fingers flying. Before it could fade, he recorded the dream, in its every detail. Such nightmares came to him regularly—often involving some terrible creature or unidentified danger. Many of the plots and characters in his novels and stories had been literally dreamed up; he would routinely rise from a bizarre nightmare and, as calmly professional as a secretary, jot down notes.

He'd had these useful nightmares for many years, ever since receiving a blow on the head during his stint as a cop in Salt Lake City. At first there had been torturous headaches, as well, but these had faded, and the dreams remained. He was quite accustomed to them, but neither of his wives nor his children had ever got used to his nocturnal thrashing and bellowing, his moans and screams frequently awakening them.

Both of his wives had insisted that he sleep in a separate bedroom.

He was right up to where the scimitar-wielding man-beast had entered the dream when another scream echoed across the night—not his own.

A woman's scream, a scream of terror, cut off abruptly!

The cry came from outside, had found its way through an open window, and seemed to be coming from the direction of the beach. He threw on the maroon robe, not even bothering to sash it, and ran barefoot into the night, finding his way through the palm trees in his backyard, toward where the purple ocean blended with the purple sky, with only the stars to show the difference, padding down onto the white sand, which looked gold in the moonlight, like the sequins on the emerald woman in his dream.

This nightmare had a woman in it, too, but Burroughs was not, unfortunately, sleeping: she lay sprawled ten or fifteen yards down the sandy expanse, lying near the surf, which rolled gently but insistently onto the shore. A man was kneeling over her, touching her shoulder with one hand, blood glistening on the other.

Burroughs could already see who the woman was: Pearl Harada, still in her blue gown, askew on her side on the sand, her skull crushed, blood turning the beach black around her ruined head. Nearby lay a blood-spattered stone, one of the thick, roundish rocks used in the luau *imu*—an impromptu weapon anyone might have picked up.

The man bending over the obviously dead girl was a handsome if pockmarked Hawaiian from her band—the trombone-playing leader, Harry Kamana.

All of this the writer took in, in a heartbeat, and then

he was running toward the kneeling man and the dead girl, yelling, "You! Don't move!"

The musician looked up sharply, his eyes wild, but he did not obey Burroughs, rather he scrambled to his feet and ran, heading down the beach.

Though Burroughs was in his sixties and his quarry in his thirties, the writer was bigger than the slight, slender Hawaiian, still in his dance-band aloha shirt, and—as it turned out—faster.

He threw himself at the fleeing musician, tackling him, bringing him down onto the sand, rolling with him until they were both in the water, where the surf licked the shore. The writer had the younger man around the knees, but Kamana squirmed out of his grasp, pulling Burroughs forward, and the writer lost his robe, was climbing to his feet in the surf in just his pajama bottoms, chest as bare as Tarzan, and Kamana tried to run again, but he was running in wet sand and didn't get very far before Burroughs slammed a fist into the man's back, nailing a kidney.

Kamana blurted a cry of pain, fell facedown, splashing into the shallow water, then flipped around and, making a shrill whining war cry, came up at Burroughs, small sharp fists flying.

The older man ducked and weaved, and threw a hard right hand into the musician's belly, doubling him over, then finished him with a left to the chin that didn't have much power, but was enough to drop the man.

"You want more, you son of a bitch?" Burroughs, looming over him, asked, breathing hard, but not as hard as the younger man.

"No . . . no. . . ." Kamana's voice was high-pitched, hoarse; he was on his hands and knees in the shallow surf.

Burroughs grabbed the man by the arm and hauled him to his feet, dragging him down the beach, heading to the bungalow.

The writer paused at the girl's body. He didn't bother to take her pulse—her skull had been caved in by that rock; her brains were showing. Rage and nausea and sorrow rose in him, a volcano of emotions threatening to erupt. He turned to the musician, wanting to throttle the bastard, but something stopped him.

The man was weeping.

# FIVE

## *Sad Song*

After the luau wound down, Hully Burroughs had been in no mood to join his sailor friends Bill Fielder and Dan Pressman in any Hotel Street excursions. Bill had been rather on the morose side—he'd learned about Colonel Fielder's displeased reaction at seeing his son and the Japanese songstress on the dance floor; and Pearl herself had begged off any after-hours date, pleading fatigue from her night on the bandstand.

This meant Bill would get plastered, while Dan would be on the prowl for dames, and in that part of town, the likely candidates served up love for a fee. Hully was interested in accompanying neither a drunk nor a tomcat, and instead headed to the Royal Hawaiian, where Harry Owens's orchestra was playing. Nobody pulled off that *hapa haole* sound better, and Hully's odds of meeting a nice young female—a tourist maybe, as the absent, much-missed Marjorie Petty had been—were far better than down at sleazy Hotel Street.

He'd gotten very lucky—not in the way the sailors on Hotel Street did, either. He danced several slow tunes with a pretty brunette named Marion Thrasher, a local girl in her early twenties out celebrating a friend's birthday. She was down-to-earth and friendly, so different from the girls in California, all of whom seemed to be aspiring actresses (expecting Hully to land them a part in a Tarzan picture!). All he'd "scored" were a few lovely if tentative smiles, some conversation and a phone number . . . but he was walking on air.

Or rather driving on air, in his father's Pierce Arrow convertible, one hand on the wheel, elbow resting on the rolled-down window, enjoying the way the stirred-up, sweetly scented breeze ruffled his hair. He loved this little low-rise city of Honolulu, which hid shyly under banyans and flowering shrubs, palm trees towering over telephone poles.

Waikiki itself was a bohemian village, increasingly given over to hotels and inns, but still with room for clapboard houses, fisherman's shacks, picket fences and vacant lots. On an evening like this—well, early morning, as it was approaching one A.M.—the sounds were unbelievably romantic, the music of strolling troubadours mingling with the benign roar of surf.

As he pulled into the moonlight-washed Niumalu parking lot, the revelry of the luau was long over, the staff's cleanup accomplished, with a few lights on in the lodge itself, but most of the bungalows—peeking from between palms—dark. He parked, headed down a crushed coral path toward the Burroughs bungalow, whistling "Sweet Leilani," jingling change and keys in his khaki pockets.

That was when he heard, coming from the beach, a man's voice—his father's voice, he could have sworn—shouting *"You! Don't move!"*

The shout conveyed an urgency, and a sense of menace, that sent Hully running down the path, and cutting through the hedges, toward the sandy shore.

By the time he got there, it was over: his father had apprehended (there could be no other word) the individual, who proved to be bandleader Harry Kamana. A bare-chested O. B. was hauling the aloha-shirt-sporting musician—who was blubbering like a baby—toward their bungalow.

Hully slowed and, approaching his father, was about to ask him what had happened when he noticed the twisted form of the girl, down a ways on the beach.

For a moment, he covered his mouth, in shock and horror; then Hully managed, "Is that . . . ?"

"It's the Japanese girl," his father affirmed. "Pearl Harada. Head crushed with a rock—I caught this son of a bitch red-handed."

Literally: the musician's right hand was damply red with blood.

"I'm going to take Harry here to our bungalow," O. B. said, holding on to the slumping, bawling musician, "and call the cops. You go alert Fred at the lodge, and have him post somebody at the crime scene, so that the body isn't disturbed."

Had the situation not been so loathsome, Hully

might have laughed. "I'll be damned, Dad," he said. "You really *were* a cop."

Burroughs nodded, and dragged Kamana off.

Hully went to the lodge and woke the manager, filling him in as they walked to the beach, where the younger Burroughs got his first close, grisly look at the beautiful dead woman with the ugly head wound, bathed in gold by an obscenely beautiful Hawaiian moon.

Manager Fred Bivens—who was in his pajama top and some trousers he'd thrown on, a heavyset genial fellow in his forties—turned away, aghast.

The tide sweeping onto the shore had a distant sound, despite its closeness, like the hoarse echo of a scream. The ocean stretched purple to the horizon, glimmering with gold, almost as lovely as this girl had been.

"Are you all right, Fred?" Hully asked, touching the man's arm.

"What a hell of a thing," Fred whispered. "What a hell of a thing... She was a sweet kid. Flirty, but sweet—and so talented... What a goddamn shame."

Hully understood and shared all these sentiments, and was not surprised by the tears in Fred's eyes.

"Can you stay here with her, Fred? Till the police come? Dad's calling them."

Fred ran a hand through his thinning brown hair, shaking his head, as if saying no, as he said, "Sure . . . sure. Poor sweet kid . . ."

"We need to keep everybody away. Dad says this is a . . . crime scene, now. So you need to keep your distance, too, Fred—don't touch her or anything."

"Don't worry."

Moments later, Hully joined his father in the bungalow. The whimpering musician was seated on O. B.'s typing chair, which had been situated in the middle of the sitting room. Kamana sat there, slumped, chin on his chest, one hand on a knee, the other hand—the bloody one—held out, palm up, as if he were trying to weigh something.

O. B.—who had thrown on an aloha shirt and some chinos but whose feet were bare—stood with his muscular arms folded, staring at the musician like a scornful genie.

"Fred's standing watch," Hully said.

"Good."

"When will the police get here?"

"Soon. I got lucky."

"How so?"

"Have you met my friend Jardine?"

Hully shook his head. "Don't believe so."

"He's a Portuguese—the best homicide detective on the island—works out of City Hall, not the police station. Officially he's a detective on the Honolulu PD, but he operates strictly out of the prosecutor's office, principally on murder cases."

"That's a good thing?"

Burroughs came over to his son, turning his back to the seated, moaning musician, and whispered, "Local PD is so corrupt, it makes the LAPD look squeaky-clean."

"Jeez."

"Jardine's straight as an arrow. Luckily he was in, at this hour."

"Why was he?"

A tiny half smile crinkled O. B.'s bronzed face. "When he isn't working a murder case, he makes a habit on weekend nights of standing at the corner of Hotel and Bishop, giving the soldiers and sailors the evil eye. He's known around there as a hard-nosed cop, so standing guard like that, looking at passersby like they're all suspects, well it's his idea of crime prevention. . . . I caught him at his desk just before he was heading home."

Hully figured this Jardine had probably given his friends Fielder and Pressman the "evil eye" tonight—and many nights.

*"I want to wash my hands!"*

Hully and his father turned toward the musician, who had finally stopped sobbing and spoken—actually, more like yelled.

O. B. went over to the man—who was holding the blood-streaked hand out, staring at it—and sneered down at him. "I just bet you'd like to wash your hands of this."

The slight, pockmarked, roughly handsome Kamana looked up, as if startled, as if realizing for the first time just what he was being accused of—even though he'd already run guiltily away. "I didn't do this."

"You didn't, huh," Burroughs said. It wasn't really a question.

Kamana's eyes were about as red as the bloody hand. "I loved her. . . . I loved her more than life!"

"More than *her* life?"

"I didn't kill her!" Though he'd stopped crying, he nonetheless seemed on the verge of hysteria. "I'd sooner kill myself!"

O. B. grunted a humorless laugh. "Maybe you'd better save it for the cops."

But Kamana wanted to talk, and the words tumbled out of him—how two years ago Pearl Harada, who had been visiting relatives in Honolulu, auditioned for his band, on an impulse. When Kamana told her she had the job, Pearl had moved from San Francisco to Oahu.

"I knew she was something special. . . . It was more than just her looks, or that nice voice of hers . . . so much like Dinah Shore . . . she had star quality. She could have gone places. *We* might have gone places!"

Hully knew what the man was doing: Kamana was talking about her because it was a way of keeping her alive. Though it seemed obvious he'd killed her, this man just as obviously was deeply sorry she was dead.

O. B. didn't seem terribly moved by any of this. "So you might have 'gone places' . . . and that makes you innocent of her murder? As in, why would you kill your meal ticket?"

Kamana was shaking his head, and he seemed desperate to be believed. "She was more than that to me . . . so much more. I didn't date her at first . . . I tried to keep things . . . businesslike. But we hit it off so well, musically, it was just natural for us to get together, in other ways. . . . I wanted her to marry me. But she wouldn't. She said her career came first, and she didn't want to settle down anyway . . . and she dated a lot of guys, mostly servicemen who followed the band. Then this Fielder came along . . . and she got serious with him . . . said she was going to marry him . . . quit the band . . . quit show business . . . quit me."

Hully asked, casually, "So you argued? Tonight?"

"We've argued several times about it," Kamana said. Talking seemed to calm him. "But not tonight. I . . . I accepted it and . . . well, I was hoping it would just . . . pass. Anyway, I figured in the long run it was just a pipe dream. . . . That Fielder kid, his colonel papa wouldn't put up with his boy marrying a Jap. I stopped arguing with her—maybe she would come to her senses, maybe she wouldn't, but that Fielder kid would . . . or at least his father would make him come to his senses."

"So," Hully said, "you were just . . . chatting tonight, down on the beach."

Kamana shook his head, emphatically. "I wasn't talking to her on the beach . . . not at all, not tonight! I heard arguing . . . my bungalow's near the beach, you know . . . and recognized her voice . . . heard a man's voice, but it was soft, I didn't recognize it. Then I . . . I heard her scream, and I ran out and down there . . . and . . ."

He began to weep again, instinctively covering his face with his hands—smearing the blood all over himself. Hully glanced at O. B., who looked back with wide eyes.

". . . She was dead. . . . My lovely Pearl was dead. . . . Somebody killed her. . . . All crushed in . . . I tried to help her, and got her blood on me. . . ."

His pockmarked face was streaked with blood, now—he looked like an Apache with war paint.

A knock at the door made them jump, even O. B., who said to Hully, "Get that."

The man Hully let in was small and swarthy, a hawk-faced obvious plainclothes cop in a snap-brim fedora, rumpled gray suit and red tie. His eyes were small and dark and needle-sharp.

"Hulbert Burroughs," Hully said, extending his hand to the little detective.

"John Jardine," he replied, and shook Hully's hand, a strong grip.

Jardine and O. B. shook hands, as well. The elder Burroughs had already filled the detective in on many of the particulars, over the phone.

"How did you get blood on your face, Mr. Kamana?" Jardine asked bluntly, standing uncomfortably close to the seated musician.

"It isn't on my face," Kamana said, stupidly, holding up his hand, where the blood was just a stain, now.

"It's on your face."

Kamana's grief had subsided and fear was moving in; with Honolulu's top homicide cop staring him down, the musician obviously was grasping what kind of spot he was in. "It . . . it was on my hand . . . I must have . . . must have touched my face. . . ."

"How did you get it on your hand?"

Hully and his father sat on the couch as Jardine questioned Kamana—just preliminary stuff, but Hully was interested in the musician's responses, which were for the most part a rehash of the things Kamana had emotionally blurted to Hully and O. B.

But Hully was impressed by the unrehearsed consistency of Kamana's answers.

Before long, Jardine was lugging Kamana—his hands cuffed behind him—outside into the breeze-kissed dark, where he turned the musician over to a uniformed cop, a Polynesian who walked Kamana toward a squad car waiting in the parking lot near the lodge. From down toward the beach came bursts of light, as if a tiny lightning storm had moved in.

Noting Hully's confused expression, Jardine said, "Flash photos."

Hully nodded—like his dad had said, the beach was a crime scene now . . . and Pearl was no longer a person, but evidence.

The Portuguese detective said to O. B., "Do you mind a few questions? While it's all fresh in your mind?"

"Not at all. Shall we go back inside?"

O. B. was opening the screen door for the detective when a figure came rushing up, dressed in white, a ghost emerging from the darkness.

Otto Kuhn—in a white shirt and white linen pants, looking like a male nurse seeking a doctor—seemed out of breath, though his bungalow, next door, was hardly any distance. His light blue eyes had a startled look.

"Are you with the police, sir?" he asked Jardine in his thick yet smoothly accented second tenor.

"I'm Detective Jardine."

"I'm Otto Kuhn—I live there." He pointed toward the bungalow past a cluster of palms. "Could I speak to you, sir?"

Jardine gestured toward the sitting room, which beckoned beyond the screen door O. B. held open. "Mr. Burroughs, do you mind?"

"Not at all."

And soon Hully and his father were again seated on the couch, spectators, as the German real-estate agent spoke excitedly to the Portuguese detective. Though Kuhn towered over the little man, literally, Jardine's commanding presence loomed over the German, figuratively.

With an inappropriate smile, Kuhn said, "I saw you arrest that . . . native. That musician."

"You did."

"Yes, and you were correct to do so. I . . . hesitated to come forward until I was sure he was safely in custody."

"You sound as if you were afraid of Kamana, Mr. Kuhn."

Kuhn swallowed, nodded. "I'm not proud to admit that is the case. You see . . . I saw of what brutality he was capable. My bungalow . . . a window looks out on the beach. It is somewhat blocked by trees, but I had them trimmed back, recently . . . for a better view."

"What kind of view did you have tonight, Mr. Kuhn?"

"I was sleeping," he said, tilting his head, as if onto a pillow, "and woke suddenly. . . ." He jerked his head straight up.

Hully winced; these histrionics were somehow distasteful.

Kuhn was saying, "I heard arguing, loud arguing, a man and a woman. I rolled over, to go back to sleep . . . my wife did not waken, I must emphasize, she saw nothing."

"All right."

Gesturing with both hands, the German said, "The arguing got louder. Heated, you might say. I went to the window, to complain. I think if I shout at them, they might stop, and I can sleep again, and no one would be harmed. But when I got to the window . . . that's when I saw it."

"Saw what?"

"The murder. That man . . . the Hawaiian musician, Kamana . . . he had something in his hand . . . a rock, I think. Something heavy, anyway, small enough for him to grasp. He raised his hand, and I wanted to shout, 'Stop!' But I was too late . . . she screamed, and he struck her. Struck her a terrible blow."

Kuhn lowered his head, shaking it, as if remembering this terrible thing . . . but something about it seemed hollow to Hully. He glanced at his father, to see if he could read any similar reaction, and noted his dad's eyes were so narrow, they might have been cuts in his face.

"This is a very interesting story, Mr. Kuhn," Jardine said. "I have one question—why didn't you call the police?"

Kuhn nodded toward O. B., on the couch. "I saw Mr. Burroughs capture the Hawaiian. . . . Edgar was obviously taking him to justice. I calmed my wife . . . she had woken by this time, and heard my story, and had become terribly upset . . . and I simply waited for you to arrive." He smiled, clasped his hands in front of him, like a waiter about to show a patron to a really nice table. "I would be most happy to give you a formal statement, tomorrow, at your headquarters."

Jardine said nothing for a few seconds; then he sighed, and said, "Why don't you show me the window you saw all this through?"

Kuhn nodded, curtly. "My pleasure."

*Pleasure?* That seemed an odd thing to say. . . . Hully found this German's story unsettling, and unconvincing, despite the way it hewed to the particulars of Pearl Harada's death.

As he accompanied Kuhn out, Jardine turned to O. B. and said, "We'll talk tomorrow, Mr. Burroughs. Thanks for your help—shouldn't have to bother you again, tonight."

"Good night, John," O. B. said, seeing them to the door.

"Nice meeting you," Jardine said to Hully, and then they were out of the door.

A few minutes later, Hully was folding the couch out into its bed, and his father—in a fresh pair of pajama bottoms—came out from his bedroom and stood there, bare-chested, with his hands on hips, Tarzan-style.

"I thought that trombone player was a killer," O. B. said, "until ol' Otto started agreeing with me."

Hully, unbuttoning his shirt, said, "Why did Kuhn

wait so long to come forward? Why didn't he come out and help you nab that guy, if he witnessed everything?"

O. B. blew a raspberry. "That Kraut didn't see a damn thing."

"Funny . . . that's my instinct, too. But why would he claim to have?"

"I don't know, son . . . I sure as hell don't know." He heaved a sigh, and hit the light switch. "Get some sleep, and we'll talk about it in the morning."

Hully lay on his back, staring up into the darkness, the breeze blowing through the window, its flowery scent suddenly seeming too sweet, sickly sweet. He thought about the musician, and how sincere the man had seemed; he thought about Kuhn, and how phony that bastard had been.

Then he thought about Pearl Harada, and thought about his friend Bill Fielder, probably sleeping off a drunk somewhere, blissfully unaware of the tragedy.

His pillow was damp, so he turned it over and, finally, went to sleep—hoping his father wouldn't awaken him with another damn nightmare.

# TWO:

## *December 6, 1941*

# SIX

## *Neighborly Visits*

Strong morning trade winds blew across Oahu, fronds of palms and plants ruffling, cane fields undulating, surf swelling, the clear sky disrupted only by smokelike puffs of clouds over the Koolau mountain range. Between that range at the east and the Waianae range at the west lay both the capital city of Honolulu and the Naval base of Pearl Harbor.

The base—though well located for a strategic deployment of the United States Navy—was a logistical nightmare, with the nearest resupply three thousand miles away on the American West Coast. Also, the one-channel entrance of the landlocked harbor could bottle up easily with the sinking of a single ship; and, even under ideal circumstances, getting the fleet out of that channel and onto the open sea required three hours. When the fleet was in—as it was on this first weekend of December—the port was clogged with ships, supply dumps, repair installations and highly flammable fuel.

Pearl Harbor might well have been designed for air attack. But a battle fleet in Hawaii was deemed necessary to deter Japan, and no alternative location could be found offering advantages and facilities to match Pearl's. Interceptor aircraft, AA guns and radar equipment would simply have to shore up the harbor's weaknesses. So said Washington and its top military minds.

Of course, Honolulu had already been invaded by air—on the previous weekend, when a silver plane circled the city before landing in Kapiolani Park, where three thousand civilians watched and screamed . . . in delight: Santa Claus had arrived. Sponsored by the *Honolulu Advertiser,* piloted by the 86th Observation Squadron, Saint Nick's invasion was part of an attempt by the city fathers to provide a more traditional—and commercial—Christmas than the underwhelming Yuletide season that was the Hawaiian norm.

With the defense boom, the city was swarming with homesick American boys—defense workers as well as servicemen—stuck in these tropical surroundings, pining for their favorite winter holiday. Sears and Roebuck responded by hanging brightly wrapped presents from the palm trees surrounding their parking lot, and festive colored lights had been strung across major streets; even the street-corner Santas—most of whom were Japanese—were putting some extra swing into their bell-ringing.

Still, it seemed rather halfhearted to Edgar Rice Burroughs, who was used to sunny Christmases, having lived in California for some time now, though his many years in the Midwest meant he knew damn well what a real white Christmas was all about. The cellophane window wreaths and tinsel-draped palms of Honolulu didn't really cut the mustard.

After last night's luau, a light breakfast seemed called for, and around nine A.M., Burroughs and Hully—in their tennis whites, rackets at hand—sat on wicker chairs at a small round wicker table on the lodge's back patio and ate fresh cut pineapple and buttered toast, and sipped coffee.

This was an exceptionally beautiful day, even for Hawaii, Burroughs noted—clear sky, sharp light, fresh air. Hard to believe, just hours before, a young woman had been murdered in such idyllic surroundings. The prospect of playing tennis, within a few yards of where her corpse had been flung, a blossom ripped roughly from a tree, seemed somehow improper . . . even sacrilegious.

"I don't feel much like tennis this morning," Hully said, returning his china cup to its dish with a slight clatter.

"I was just thinking the same thing."

His son's brow furrowed. "Your friend . . . Detective Jardine . . ."

"Yes?"

"You respect him? He's a good cop?"

Burroughs sipped his coffee, raised an eyebrow. "Probably the best investigator on this island—that's why I called him, sought him out specifically. . . . That and his honesty."

"So . . . the case is in good hands."

Burroughs said nothing.

"Dad?"

A few of the tables nearby were taken up by other Niumalu guests. From the expressions on various faces, it was clear that news of the murder had gotten around—and judging by the occasional glances he and Hully were getting, their participation in the discovery of the body was common knowledge . . . or anyway, common gossip.

"Let's take a walk, Hully—let's return to the scene of the crime."

Within a few minutes, after depositing their tennis rackets at their bungalow, along with their abandoned thoughts of a morning round or two, father and son were sitting on the sand—the beach again a beach, a crime scene no more, though one ominous blackened area, like a scab on the sand, was marked by the victim's dried blood. The steady rush of the surf, the understated thunder of it, might have been soothing—under other circumstances.

Hully sat like an Indian, while Burroughs had his bronzed, muscular legs sticking straight out, his palms on the sand, bracing him.

"Normally I would be content to leave this to John Jardine," Burroughs said, voice barely audible above the surf. "But John's only flaw, if it is one, has to do with his working out of the prosecutor's office."

"I don't understand."

Burroughs twitched a half smile. "Jardine's specialty isn't so much solving a crime as providing an airtight case for his boss to take into court. He'll dig in and do the legwork, all the tedious stuff real detectives do . . . but he'll do it all operating from the assumption that that musician did the murder."

Hully shrugged. "It does look open-and-shut. Kamana had motive, opportunity . . ."

"Blood on his hands." Burroughs tossed a pebble at the tide, raised a single eyebrow. "That's the problem: I'm afraid Jardine won't do anything except dig into Harry Kamana—and until or unless he finds out that Kamana didn't do the murder, nobody else will get looked at as a suspect."

Both Hully's eyebrows had climbed his forehead. "Is that what you think? That Kamana is innocent?"

"What's your opinion?"

Hully sighed, and stared out at the vast blue of the sky meeting the ocean. He was a handsome young man—Burroughs could see so much of his own late mother in the boy's sensitive, oval face.

"Well, like you said last night, O. B.—Kamana was a hell of a lot more credible than that Kuhn character . . . but why would Kuhn have lied?"

"Maybe he did the killing." Burroughs nodded to the left, toward the foliage lining the beach, behind which the German's bungalow nestled. "He had easy access— as you put it, opportunity."

Hully was making a face. "What's his motive?"

"Pearl was a nice girl, but let's face it—she got around. And Otto, married or not, has a reputation as a playboy."

Hully snapped his fingers. "That makes his wife a

suspect, too! Suppose Otto and Pearl were down on the beach, and Mrs. Kuhn caught 'em!"

Nodding, with a wry, rueful smile, Burroughs said, "Doesn't take long to come up with other suspects, does it? And there could be other reasons why Kuhn lied."

"If he did lie."

"If he did lie," Burroughs allowed. He wanted to share Kuhn's supposed status as "sleeper" agent for the Japanese; but didn't feel he should betray FBI agent Sterling's confidence.

"Anyway, I can see the problem with Jardine," Hully said. "As a prosecutor's investigator, he's already focused on one suspect—when there are plenty of others."

Burroughs glanced around, to make sure he and his son were still alone on the beach. "I hate to say so, but . . . Colonel Fielder *and* his son have to be included on that list."

Hully was shaking his head. "I can't believe Bill would do anything to harm Pearl—he was crazy about her!"

" 'Crazy' might be the operative word—suppose *Bill* found Pearl with another man, on the beach?"

"Well . . . I can see your point, but—"

"Were you with Bill last night? Can you alibi him?"

Hully lowered his gaze. "No. Last I saw him, he was on Hotel Street . . . plenty of time to get back here."

"And I know for a fact Pearl was looking to talk to Fielder. . . ."

Quickly, Burroughs filled his son in on Pearl's visit

to the bungalow, and her request for Burroughs to set up a meeting with Bill's father.

"She asked me the same thing," Hully said. "Wanted me, or you, to arrange a meet. Are you thinking the colonel may have come back . . . or was still hanging around here . . . and she approached him, and . . . tried to present her case, for marrying Bill, and . . ."

"Can you deny it's a possibility?"

Hully gestured with an open hand. "What if you run all of this by Jardine?"

"I intend to . . . but I know how that Portuguese police dog's mind works, and I know his single-minded technique."

"What do you suggest, Dad?"

Burroughs leaned toward his son, placed a hand on Hully's shoulder, gently squeezing. "Why don't we do a little . . . informal investigating? We can chat with people—many of the suspects are our friends, after all. . . ."

"Unfortunately."

"No—fortunately." Now Burroughs looked out at the ocean and the sky, his eyes, his whole face, tight as a clenched fist. "The worst that could be said of that young woman is she may have been a little fast. She didn't deserve anything but a long, happy life. She was pretty and smart and talented. Any 'friend' of mine who murdered that girl is no friend at all."

"Dad . . . Jesus, Dad. You really *were* a cop."

He turned to Hully again. "What do you say, son? Why don't we split up, and do some . . . socializing?"

Hully's eyes narrowed, then he nodded, vigorously. "Pearl deserves our help."

"She sure as hell does—I only wish I'd been a little earlier last night, and could have really helped her, when she needed it most."

They briefly discussed who among the Niumalu residents and staff each would attempt to interrogate—without seeming to, of course—and soon Hully was heading off toward the lodge, and Burroughs was angling over toward the bungalow where the Kuhns resided.

As he approached, he encountered Mrs. Fujimoto, coming from the direction of the Kuhn bungalow. The slender, fortyish kimono-clad woman, her graying hair tucked back in a bun, worked as a maid at the Niumalu; she was not on the hotel staff, rather worked for a handful of guests who shared her services, Burroughs and the Kuhns among them.

"Good morning, Mr. Burroughs," she said, stopping, lowering her head respectfully.

"How are you this morning, Mrs. Fujimoto?"

"Very sad, since I hear of Miss Pearl Harada's misfortune. Very sad."

Nodding, Burroughs said, "She was a lovely girl, a nice person—she'll be missed."

Mrs. Fujimoto looked up and her eyes were filigreed red; she wore no makeup, which made her seem rather plain when actually her features were pleasant. "I am on way to your cottage, Mr. Burroughs, to begin my work."

He checked his watch. "You're not due till around eleven, are you?"

"I run early—the Kuhns did not want me . . . what they say? 'Underfoot.' Is it inconvenience, my early come?"

"No, no—go ahead."

At the Kuhns' bungalow, Burroughs stood on the stoop at the screen door, about to knock, when the German opened the door, slapping the writer with it.

"Sorry, Edgar!" Kuhn looked aghast. "Forgive me!"

Burroughs, knocked back a bit, touched his forehead and said, "Jeez, Otto, where's the fire?"

"Fire?" Shutting the screen, Kuhn joined the writer, at the bottom of the short stoop. The German was again in white linen, his tie a light blue, damn near matching the light blue of his eyes—the whiteness of his suit was stark against the rose-colored bougainvillea blanketing his bungalow.

Burroughs explained, " 'Where's the fire'—what's your hurry?"

Kuhn blinked, raised his chin. "Oh, I have a business appointment." Then he put a hand on the writer's shoulder. "I feel the fool—are you all right?"

"I'll survive." Actually, the wooden frame had clipped Burroughs on the forehead and it did hurt, a little. "I just wanted to see how you were doing, this morning—after that unpleasantness last night."

Kuhn withdrew his hand from Burroughs's shoulder, and summoned an unconvincing smile; it was like a gash in his pasty pale face. "How thoughtful, Edgar. Well, of course, it was a terrible thing to witness." He said this as offhandedly as a man describing an over-cooked steak he'd had to send back.

Burroughs shook his head. "I should say—her scream woke me from a deep sleep, and scared the bejesus out of me." That wasn't exactly true, but the writer liked the effect of it. "Did Pearl scream when Kamana raised the rock?"

Kuhn cocked his head. "Pardon me?"

"Well, you saw the murder—did she scream when Kamana raised his hand, to strike her? Or did he hit her more than once, and she screamed after one glanc-ing blow . . . and then another blow, or blows, silenced her?"

The blue eyes were wide, white showing all around. "I, uh . . . my God, Edgar, this is an unpleasant subject. I've already had to go over this with the police, again and again . . . I was up until all hours."

Burroughs raised his palms, as if in surrender. "My mistake—I thought, since we'd both been witnesses to this thing, that we had something in common. That we'd shared something, however horrible."

Kuhn nodded, once. "I do understand—I meant no offense. But I would prefer not to discuss the matter any further."

Not the murder—the "matter."

"Sure, Otto. I guess I don't blame you."

The ambiguity of what Burroughs had just said froze the German for a moment; then he gave the writer an-other curt nod. "If you'll excuse me, Edgar—I have business downtown."

Kuhn strode off across the grass, toward the lodge

and its parking lot, and Burroughs began back toward his own quarters; then, when Kuhn was out of sight, the writer cut back toward the bougainvillea-covered bungalow.

He didn't have to knock on the screen door, this time—Kuhn's wife, the person he had hoped to casually interview, was already outside. He didn't see her, at first—she was down at the far end of the bungalow, tucked back in the cool blue shade of sheltering palms, seated in a wood-and-canvas beach-type chair.

Elfriede Kuhn's slender shape was well served by a white halter top and matching shorts. Honey-blonde hair brushing her shoulders, eyes a mystery behind the dark blue circles of white-framed sunglasses, she sat slumped with the back of her head resting on the wooden chair, using both armrests, her legs stretched out, ankles crossed. Her thin, wide, pretty mouth was red with lipstick, but otherwise she wore no makeup that he could detect.

She was a handsome woman of perhaps forty-five, but she looked better from a distance.

Perhaps she was staying out of the sun because her flesh had already passed the merely tanned stage into dark leather, and her high-cheekboned face—which most likely had, in her twenties and probably thirties, rivaled that of any fashion model—bore a crinkly, weathered look.

"Mr. Burroughs," she said, as he wandered into sight. She had a cigarette in a clear holder in one hand and a half-empty glass of orange juice in the other. "If you're looking for a tennis partner, I'm afraid I'm simply too tired."

She spoke with only the faintest German accent.

"I'm in no mood myself, Mrs. Kuhn. May I join you for a moment? It looks cool there in the shade."

"Certainly." She gestured to another beach chair, near the side of the house. "I can go in and get you one of these."

She was lifting the orange-juice glass; he was dragging the chair around, to sit beside her.

"No thanks," he said. "I've had my breakfast."

"Ah, but this isn't just breakfast. It's a rejuvenating tonic known as a screwdriver."

He grinned a little, shook his head. "No thanks— I'm on the wagon . . . holding on by my thumbs, but holding on. . . . Little early for that, isn't it?"

She sipped from the glass. "Is it ever too early for vitamin C? Or vodka? Citrus is rich in it, you know. Vitamin C, that is."

"Yeah, I know—I used to live in California. Plenty of citrus. And vodka."

Mrs. Kuhn blew a smoke ring, regally. "I would love to live in California. I have had more than enough of . . . paradise."

"But your husband has his business here."

"Yes. Oh yes."

Burroughs shifted in the canvas seat. "I ran into him a few minutes ago, on his way to some business appointment or other. He didn't say what, exactly."

She said nothing; she might not even have been listening. The wind was rippling the fronds overhead, making gently percussive music, while underneath the sibilant rush of the nearby surf provided its monotonous melody.

"Terrible thing, last night," Burroughs said.

She nodded, almost imperceptibly. "You caught the murderer, I understand."

"I heard a scream. Ran out to the beach. That musician was leaning over the poor girl's body, blood on his hands."

"Awful," she said emotionlessly.

"What did you hear?"

"Pardon?"

"When did you wake up?"

She turned her head toward him and lowered her sunglasses and her pale blue eyes studied him; her thin lips curved in mild amusement. "Is this really the proper subject for casual midmorning conversation?"

"No disrespect meant, to either you or the deceased." He shrugged. "It's just that . . . you and I and your husband, we're the only witnesses to this tragedy."

She frowned and turned away, put her sunglasses back into position. "I'm not a witness, Mr. Burroughs. I didn't wake up until my husband's . . . activity awoke me."

"Activity?"

"He was quite understandably agitated by what he saw."

"So he woke you."

She heaved an irritated sigh and looked at him again, not bothering to lower the sunglasses, this time. "Really, Mr. Burroughs, this is nothing I want to talk about—I spent half the night blathering with that dreadful little foreign policeman, and I don't want to gossip about such a misfortune with a neighbor—*if you don't mind.*"

"I meant no offense."

"Neither did I."

She wasn't looking at him, now—neither one of their apologies had sounded very convincing.

He shrugged again. "It just rather casts a pall over this lovely day."

"You can have this lovely day, and every other lovely Hawaiian day, as far as I'm concerned."

"Pearl Harada might not agree with you."

"What is that supposed to mean?"

"It means she had *every* day taken away from her . . . and it wasn't her idea. That's all it means."

She sipped the screwdriver. "I'm sorry the young woman is dead, but I barely knew her."

"You did know her, though."

"I knew her as any guest at the Niumalu knew her—she was an entertainer, here—a decent one, too. She seemed pleasant enough, when I would encounter her around the place. Not stuck-up like some show-business types. I'm sorry she's gone." She looked at him over the rims of the sunglasses. "Is there anything else, Mr. Burroughs?"

"I apologize, Mrs. Kuhn—I was just making conversation. I thought . . . as mutual witnesses . . . we had something in common."

"You said that. Mr. Burroughs, if you'd like to go get your tennis racket, I'll meet you on the court. Or

if you'd like to sit here and share some stories about
the Hollywood celebrities you've encountered, please
feel welcome. Otherwise, change the subject, or find
someone else to gossip with."

He rose. "Sorry, Mrs. Kuhn. And I'm still in no
mood for tennis, and I like talking about Hollywood
about as much as you like discussing murder. . . . Have
you seen Mr. Sterling this morning?"

The FBI man's bungalow was the next one over, the
only other bungalow near enough to the beach for
someone within to have possibly heard or seen something last night.

"Yes, I have—he chatted with Otto this morning, on
this same dreadful subject. Then he headed off."

Burroughs frowned. "Do you know where he went?"

Her patience clearly all but exhausted, Mrs. Kuhn
said, "I believe Mr. Sterling said he was going in to
work."

"Oh . . . well, thanks, Mrs. Kuhn. Sorry—didn't
mean to disturb you with this unpleasantness."

"I'm sure," she said, coldly. "Just as I did not mean
to be rude."

Burroughs headed over to the lodge, to catch up with
Hully, mind abuzz. It was unusual for the FBI man to
work on a Saturday morning, and he and Sterling were
set to go to the Shriners game this afternoon, with Colonel Fielder. He wondered if Sterling's Saturday-
morning business had anything to do with Pearl
Harada's murder.

He wondered the same about Otto Kuhn's business
downtown.

# SEVEN

## *Mourning After*

Hully drifted through an open archway into the airy, A-frame lobby of the Niumalu, its sun-reflecting parquet floor dotted with Oriental rugs, potted ferns perching on the periphery like silent witnesses. Nary a guest was partaking of the cushioned wicker chairs and sofas, but manager Fred Bivens was behind the front desk of the lodge, at the far end, distributing mail into key slots.

Fred's aloha shirt was an all-purpose blue on which floated the fluffy clouds and palmy island of its pattern. The affable, heavyset Bivens put aside his work to chat with Hully—the manager's eyes were dark and baggy, his normally pleasant features seeming to droop, as if last night's tragedy had melted his face slightly.

"How late did the cops keep you up last night?" Bivens asked.

Their voices echoed in the high-ceilinged room.

"Not as late as some," Hully said. "Dad and I were the first questioned . . . us and Harry Kamana. Did they wake up a lot of your guests, for questioning?"

"No, just the residents in the bungalows adjacent to the beach. But that little Puerto Rican cop said he'd be back either today or Monday, to talk to everybody else."

Hully didn't correct Bivens's assumption about Jardine's ethnicity. "You have any guests checking out before then?"

"That cop asked the same thing—no. We're about half and half, at the moment, residents like you and your father, and tourists . . . but nobody's leaving before the middle of next week."

Hully leaned an arm on the counter. He was trying to keep things conversational—he didn't want the manager to figure out he was poking around. Then he shook his head and said, "Damn shame—I really liked Pearl. I know she dated a lot of guys, but I never got the feeling she was . . . ."

"Round-heeled or anything? No. I don't think she was any virgin, but she wasn't any, you know . . . tramp. She was a good kid, with a good heart; but hell, all those show-business types have different moral codes than the rest of us."

"How so?"

Now Bivens leaned on the counter. "Come on, Hully—you and your dad live in Hollywood. You know how those movie actors sleep around; you know how those musicians drink and smoke . . . and I'm not talking about cigarettes."

Hully shrugged. "I didn't have the feeling Pearl wanted to stay in show business. Matter of fact, she told me she wanted to get married and settle down."

Bivens's head rocked back. "What, with that Fielder kid? Come on, Hully—that was a pipe dream! White soldier with a high-ranking father, marry a Jap?"

"Yeah," Hully admitted, "it was a loaded situation. . . . I wonder if that had anything to do with her murder."

Bivens started filling the mail slots again, talking as he did, occasionally glancing back at Hully. "Sure it did. That poor Kamana musta gone off his noodle, with jealousy. He loved that girl—everybody knew it."

"Does Harry Kamana seem like the violent type to you, Fred? You ever see him lose his temper?"

"No. . . . That's the pity. He's always been a sweet guy. But still waters run deep." He paused, several letters in hand, and his gaze held Hully's. "Funny thing, that. He's the leader, you know, of the Harbor Lights, and some of his guys have come to me to complain."

"What about?"

Letters distributed, he folded his arms, leaned against the back counter. "Well, they know I do the deals with Harry . . . book the gigs, as they put it. And they think I take advantage of Harry . . . that he's too nice, too soft."

"Any truth in it?"

"Hey, I give the boys a fair shake. They get pretty close to top dollar, for the size of the Niumalu and its dance floor."

"They're popular—a real draw."

Bivens shook his head, sadly. "Without Pearl...
without Harry... I don't know. They're having a
meeting right now, over in the dining room. I don't
know what the hell they're gonna do.... Supposed to
play for me, tonight."

The musicians were in the dining room, up on the
bandstand, casually dressed, sitting in their respective
seats in front of music stands; but they weren't rehears-
ing—no instruments were in sight.

A guy in a dark blue sportshirt and chinos was standing in front of them, as if directing—but he was really
just conducting a meeting. Hully knew him, knew most
of the remaining eight members of the Harbor Lights;
the guy out front was Jim Kaupiko, a round-faced but
slender trumpet player in his late twenties. Most tourists assumed the entire band was Hawaiian, and Kaupiko and Kamana and a few other Harbor Lights were
indeed natives; but the band was otherwise a mix of
Japanese, Chinese, Filipino and Korean.

"I know how everybody here feels," Kaupiko said.
"Pearl was the best..."

The various Polynesian and Oriental faces on the
bandstand were as grave as carved masks.

"... and we can't ever hope to find someone to fill
her shoes. Whether we're even gonna be able to keep
going, that's up in the air. But we owe it to Mr. Bivens
to play out our contract, at least."

"Including tonight?" a voice called out.

"Including tonight, Terry."

Hully knew the band member who had spoken: Taro

"Terry" Mizuha, the only Japanese in the group other than Pearl.

"I don't know, Jim," Mizuha said, shaking his head. A slender, almost pretty young man—a guitar player— he really looked devastated. "I just don't know. . . ."

"I've asked Sally Suziki to fill in on vocals—she was singing with the Kealoha Trio at the Halekulani, but they recently broke up."

"She'll do fine," somebody said numbly.

"She's no Pearl," somebody else said.

"She'll do fine," Kaupiko affirmed. "And I've got Sammy Amaulu, trombone player from the Surfriders— they're not gigging tonight. Sammy can fill in, but just this once."

Somebody asked, "Are we gonna rehearse with these fill-ins?"

"Today at three—any objections?"

There were none, and Kaupiko seemed about to ad-journ the informal meeting, when Hully strolled up and said, "What do you guys think about Harry?"

About half of them had been getting up out of their chairs; all of them had wide-eyed, sucker-punched ex-pressions.

Kaupiko, still in the director's position on the band-stand, turned and looked down and said, "Hiya, Hully— heard you and your old man found Pearl, and nabbed Harry."

"It was mostly Dad's doing. . . . I just wondered what you guys thought, you know, about whether Harry did it or not."

One of the guys, a Filipino whose name Hully didn't

know, a sax player, asked, "I thought your father caught him red-handed."

"Red-handed in that he had blood on his hand . . . but maybe it got there 'cause he was trying to help her, or check the pulse in her neck. I just thought you guys should know that Harry denied killing Pearl—he could probably use some support about now. Somebody ought to go downtown and make sure he's got a good lawyer."

"Sounds like he'll need one," Kaupiko said.

"No question about that. But I thought maybe you fellas . . . his friends . . . would like to know that I, for one, found his story convincing."

"I can't believe Harry'd hurt a fly," Jack Wong said. He was also a sax player.

"He was crazy about Pearl," somebody else chimed in.

"Most people think his loving her is a motive," Hully said. "I'd just like to know if any of you guys ever saw Harry act violent—ever behave like a hothead, blow his top over anything."

Nobody said anything; everybody was sitting down again, and the band members exchanged glances, often shaking their heads.

Hully stood with hands on his hips. "How about Harry saying anything about Bill Fielder muscling in on him? Did Harry ever have a shouting match with Pearl, over that or anything else?"

No one said a word.

Hully searched the cheerless faces. "I'm not a cop . . . I'm just a friend of Harry's, who wants to make sure he doesn't get a raw deal outta this."

"Harry hardly ever raises his voice," Wong said. "That's his problem—we'd be playing at the Royal Hawaiian right now, with the following we got, if he was more aggressive."

Wong's fellow band members were nodding.

"Okay, guys," Hully said, easily. "Listen, I'll be over at my bungalow, for a while, if anybody wants to share anything, one to one, man to man. Okay?"

More nods.

Hully turned and headed out, to the tune of chairs getting pushed back and murmuring among the members.

Kaupiko caught up with him about halfway across the dance floor, taking Hully by the arm. "Let's talk," the trumpet player said, and nodded toward the courtyard, which the dining room opened onto.

The rock garden at the center had a little waterfall which made just enough noise to give them some additional privacy.

"Are you investigating Pearl's murder?" Kaupiko asked, his expression thoughtful.

"Not officially," Hully said. "But I think there's at least a possibility that Harry Kamana is innocent, and I don't see the police going down that path."

"And if Harry's innocent, somebody else is . . ."

"The word is 'guilty,' Jim. Yes." Hully rocked back on his heels. "How many of the band live here at the Niumalu?"

The round-faced musician stroked his chin, which was almost as blue as his shirt—he needed a shave.

"Besides Harry, and Pearl? Just a couple. Most are local. Harry's from the big island, though, and needs lodging when we work Oahu, which lately has been most of the time."

"I had the idea that Pearl lived with her uncle, that grocer, in Chinatown."

Kaupiko nodded. "She did, when she first came here. But once we got this steady gig at the Niumalu, Harry negotiated with Mr. Bivens to get her a room in the lodge."

"Who else lives here at the hotel?"

The musician looked around, rather furtively, apparently checking to see if any of his band mates were watching . . . or listening.

"Terry Mizuha," he said, finally. "He's the only guy besides Harry that was really cozy with Pearl."

"Did she date him, too?"

Kaupiko laughed.

"What's so funny, Jim?"

"Sorry." The musician's expression was sober again. "Listen, I don't want to talk outta school. Terry's a great guy, helluva guitar player."

"Okay—now drop the other shoe."

He shrugged. "I don't think Terry likes dolls. He's, uh . . . you know." Kaupiko held up his hand and made a sideways shaking gesture.

"But he and Pearl were friends?"

"Yeah. Sort of . . . 'girlfriends.' Hey, don't spread that around. We don't care about Terry's tastes—he's discreet and he's a good musician and he's our pal. Anyway, some of the people we work for might not hire us if they knew he was that way. So mum's the word."

"I appreciate you leveling with me, Jim."

Kaupiko sighed, shook his head. "We all loved Pearl. She could've taken us to Hollywood or somethin', someday, if some bastard hadn't done her in. And I want to thank you for saying what you did in front of the band—you really got everybody thinking. I mean, in our hearts we didn't believe Harry could have done that terrible thing . . . but we believed what we were told."

"That's understandable."

He sighed again, relieved this time. "Anyway, I'm going down to the police station and see about Harry— like you suggested."

"Good. Before you go, is there anything else you can think of, that might be pertinent?"

Kaupiko's eyes squeezed tight in thought. "Come to think of it . . . I did see Pearl have an argument last night, but not with Harry. Before we went onstage."

Hully leaned in. "Who with?"

"Do you know that Japanese diplomat, that idiot skirt-chaser Morimura?"

"I know who he is—he sat with Dad and me at the luau."

Kaupiko nodded. "Well, he had her cornered, out in the parking lot, away from everybody and everything, out by that big fancy car of his—it's a Lincoln. He was really chewing her out, shaking his finger at her. . . . She just had her arms folded and was taking it, chin up, kinda proud."

"Huh," Hully grunted. "What did you make of that?"

Kaupiko shrugged elaborately. "I didn't know what to think, and I never said a word to Pearl about it. I mean, I always thought that Morimura character was just a harmless grinning jerk, always chasing tail."

"You think Pearl and Morimura may have dated?"

Another, less elaborate shrug. "I suppose anything is possible. But it doesn't ring true, somehow. Morimura doesn't seem her type—she liked musicians, and she liked servicemen . . . that was about it. And that's the only time I ever saw them together."

"Okay."

Kaupiko gestured with a pointing finger. "If that cop asks me about this, I'm gonna tell him, too."

"Good. It's not a competition—in fact, say and do anything you can that will help get that guy Jardine off the dime, and looking at some suspects besides Harry Kamana."

The two men shook hands, and Kaupiko headed back toward the bandstand, while Hully returned to the lobby, intending to ask Bivens which room was Terry Mizuha's, wanting to talk to the guitar player.

But Bivens was no longer behind the front desk, apparently off doing some other Niumalu chore. That was all right—it was even good—because Hully didn't need Bivens's help to find Terry Mizuha.

The slender musician was sitting on a cushioned wicker chair, between two archways that looked out onto the parking lot.

Mizuha, in a cream sportshirt and white slacks and cream slippers, had almost delicate features—handsome but vaguely feminine, his dark hair long, slicked back like an Oriental George Raft. His long-lashed eyes were dark-circled and webbed with red.

"I hoped you might come through here," Mizuha said. His voice was soft, gentle, melodic.

Hully pulled another of the wicker chairs up. "Why didn't you stop me in the other room, Terry, when I asked for information?"

"Jim beat me to it. What did he tell you?"

"That you and Pearl were good friends."

"That's true . . . that's true." He covered his face with a finely boned hand and began to weep.

Hully, embarrassed, dug out a hankie from his pocket and handed it to the man, who took it gratefully; for two excruciatingly long minutes, Mizuha wept into Hully's cloth.

When the slender man lowered the handkerchief from his face, his eyes were even more bloodshot. He said, "She was my *best* friend."

"Do you know anything about her murder?"

"I know I saw that soldier . . . Stanton? She had dated him, before the sailor boy—Fielder? I saw him yelling at her, after the dance, when we were packing up."

"Did the others see this? Why didn't they—?"

Mizuha was shaking his head. "They didn't see the argument. It was outside, he had her up against the wall of the lodge. I . . . I interceded. He almost struck me, but I pretended she was needed by Jim, for band business. Stanton stalked off."

"Did you hear anything of what was said?"

"Just the usual spurned-lover recriminations."

"Did Stanton threaten her?"

"Not overtly. Just his manner. I do think she was afraid . . . she was trembling. I put my arm around her." He began to cry again, into the hankie.

Hully waited, then asked, "Is there anything else you saw, Terry? Anything else you know?"

Mizuha blinked. "What do you mean . . . anything else I know?"

This seemed a peculiar reaction to Hully, who shrugged. "Just that."

The pretty eyes narrowed; the smooth forehead furrowed. "You're not a detective, are you?"

"Unfortunately, no—just a friend trying to help a friend who is beyond help, really."

He swallowed, nodded. "You were going to talk to Colonel Fielder for her, weren't you?"

"Yes. . . . My father agreed, also."

Mizuha sat forward, a strange urgency in his voice. "What did she say to you? What did she tell you? Or your father?"

The intensity of the man made Hully rear back, a little. "Nothing, really—obviously, she wanted to state her case, plead for the colonel's consent to the marriage."

Mizuha's eyes tightened, but otherwise he relaxed, air escaping as if from a balloon, his body becoming even smaller. Then he said, "Let us talk again."

"Sure."

"I have . . . I have to sort a few things out. I have to think."

"Terry, if you know something, tell me, hell, tell the *police.* . . ."

Mizuha was shaking his head. "I'm too distraught right now. I'm confused. I'm afraid. Please give me a few hours. . . . We'll talk again."

"Terry . . ."

But the conversation ended there, because something attracted Hully's attention: he saw Bill Fielder getting out of a gray Ford sedan (it belonged to Colonel Fielder), having just parked in the Niumalu lot.

Something was terribly wrong: Bill was smiling, his expression cheerful; the young Naval officer—who was in a green sportshirt and chinos, on this fine off-duty day—was even whistling a tune.

"We'll talk more, later," Hully said, and Terry Mizuha was getting up and going off in one direction, as Hully—shuddering as if from cold on this warm morning—moved through that open archway into the parking lot, where he approached Bill, catching him before he entered the lodge.

"Hey, Hully." The handsome, cleft-chinned Fielder wore a winning smile. "Hell of a beautiful day, huh?"

"Yeah, Bill—nice weather, even for Hawaii." He touched his friend's arm. "You doing okay?"

"Yeah, better today. I skipped Hotel Street, and had it out with Dad, and . . ."

Hully stopped listening to his optimistic friend, his own mind throbbing with the inescapable realization that *Bill did not know about the murder.* . . .

"We have to sit down," Hully said, guiding his confused friend into the lodge lobby, "and we have to talk."

"What's wrong with you? What the hell—listen, I have to see Pearl, she's waiting, I'm a little late. . . ."

"Sit down, Bill. I have to tell you something—something very bad. Very sad."

Hully sat his friend down in the wicker chair the musician had vacated and he stood in front of his friend and quickly, calmly, as gently as he could, told Bill Fielder that Pearl Harada had been murdered.

Bill's cry of emotional pain echoed through the lodge like that of a mortally wounded beast.

The young Naval officer fell onto the parquet floor and assumed a fetal position and Hully got down there with him, taking his friend into his arms, patting him on the back, comforting him as Bill howled and wept. Hully couldn't even offer Bill a handkerchief because the trumpet player had taken it.

But no handkerchief could have contained the tears of the young sailor.

It was a long time before Bill got settled down enough to begin asking questions about the particulars.

Then, suddenly, the brawny officer was on his feet. "Harry Kamana? *Harry Kamana* did this? Where the hell is the bastard? I'll break his goddamn neck—"

Hully held him by the arm. "The police have Kamana, Bill—he may not have done it. He says he didn't."

But Bill didn't want to hear about that. He pulled away from Hully, ran out to the car, and tore away, throwing crushed coral like rice at a wedding.

Hully wondered what the hell good Bill thought he could do, what sort of revenge he could take, with Kamana behind bars.

He also wondered if there was the remotest possibility that his friend was good enough an actor to have concocted this entire scene—because if Bill were the murderer of Pearl Harada, he would've had to have done that very thing.

# EIGHT

## *Halftime*

The Termite Palace—as locals affectionately if accurately referred to the wooden-bleachered Honolulu Stadium—had hosted Bing Crosby concerts, championship boxing matches, and even a notorious race between Olympic runner Jesse Owens and a horse (Owens won). The unprepossessing facility—at the *ewa* (west)/*makai* (seaward) corner of King and Isenberg streets—was also home to every Oahu sporting event from club baseball to college football games, like today's annual Shriner-sponsored contest.

The stands were packed, over twenty-five thousand in attendance—10 percent of the city's population—which was unusual: college games were usually lucky to draw half that many fans. The big local attraction was high-school football, the eight-team league an Oahu obsession, fueled by gambling interests whose weekly betting turnover was said to be half a million dollars.

Burroughs found the casual corruption of Honolulu at once amusing and disturbing. To a writer, the irony of sin in paradise was appealing, and he disliked the legislation of morality; but the town's wide-open gambling and unfettered red-light district jarred his conservative Midwestern sensibilities.

Somehow the rollickingly enthusiastic crowd— watching the game for its own sake (little betting attended college games)—gave Burroughs a lift. He was enjoying this exceptionally beautiful day with its clear sky and sharp sunlight as much as anyone in the polyglot assemblage, which contained more than its share of high-ranking military personnel, including Colonel Kendall "Wooch" Fielder, next to whom the writer sat. As the first half neared its conclusion, with the Roaring Rainbows of the University of Hawaii leading the Bearcats of Willamette (Oregon) University fourteen to nothing, the reserved seat on the other side of Burroughs—meant for FBI agent Adam Sterling—was vacant.

Sterling was a rabidly loyal Willamette grad, who for weeks had been vocal about looking forward to this game, and his missing-in-action status nagged at Burroughs, who was aware the agent had taken off early this morning to go in to work. The writer could not help but again wonder if Sterling's absence was related to the murder of Pearl Harada.

When Burroughs had returned to his bungalow, this morning—after his conversations first with Otto Kuhn and then with Elfriede Kuhn—he had come in on Mrs. Fujimoto, who was, in her pastel floral kimono, vacuuming the sitting room. He had directed her to continue working, got himself a bottle of Pepsi from their little refrigerator perched in one corner, slipped his shoes off and lounged on the couch, with his feet up on it, to stay out of the maid's way.

Though Mrs. Fujimoto was invariably, subserviently formal in her manner, she and Burroughs were friendly—he often kidded her, prodding giggles out of her—and her college-boy son Sam and Hully were good pals. As he waited for Hully, Burroughs formed a few questions which he realized the maid might decline to answer . . . but were definitely worth a try.

When she had finished her vacuuming and began her feather-dusting, Burroughs said, causally, "So the Kuhns chased you out early, today."

She smiled and nodded, carefully dusting his work area.

"Mr. Kuhn almost knocked me down," Burroughs said, still lounging on the sofa, keeping his tone light. "The way he came bolting out of that bungalow, I thought he might be . . . mad or something."

She nodded. "Mr. Kuhn very upset this morning."

"Really? Well, you know, he witnessed that murder last night."

Mrs. Fujimoto looked up from her work. "I did hear this. . . . So sad." She sighed, shook her head. "Miss Pearl, so beautiful."

"It was a terrible tragedy. . . . Kuhn identified Harry Kamana as the killer, you know."

She nodded, dusting. "That I also hear. Hard to believe."

"Why do you say that?"

She dusted some more, before answering. "Mr. Kamana . . . he is a very gentle man. Kind man. He always treat Miss Pearl with kindness."

The opinion of an "invisible" person like a maid, here at the Niumalu—who observed much, from the sidelines—was not to be undervalued.

Burroughs rose, crossed to her at his desk. Her eyes widened—she was surprised by this familiarity.

Facing her, close to her, he said, his tone serious now, "I don't believe Harry Kamana killed that young woman. Do you?"

She winced. "If Mr. Kuhn say he saw it . . ."

"People lie sometimes, don't they, Mrs. Fujimoto? Were the Kuhns arguing this morning? The way he came flying out of there, that was the impression I got."

From her expression, she seemed to be experiencing physical pain. "Oh, Mr. Burroughs . . . do not ask, please. It would be improper for me to—"

"It would be improper to let Harry Kamana take the blame for something he didn't do. My son and I are looking into this matter."

"But . . . the police . . ."

"They've already made their minds up that Harry did it—largely because of what Kuhn told them. . . . Did you hear anything this morning, Mrs. Fujimoto, before the Kuhns chased you out of there? Anything . . . suspicious?"

She raised her hand, in a gentle "stop" gesture. "Mr. Burroughs . . ."

"Please."

She swallowed. Shaking her head, her gaze lowered, she said softly, "They did argue. I . . . I did not hear much."

"What *did* you hear?"

"Something . . . something about a phone call . . . a phone call last night."

*What the hell?*

Burroughs leaned in, even closer. "A phone call— what about it?"

"Mr. Kuhn tell her this phone call—it never came."

His mind was racing. "There was a phone call, but if anybody asked, she was to say there wasn't any phone call? Is that it?"

"I cannot say. I tell you what I hear. I do not understand what it mean. Please . . . Mr. Burroughs . . . I am uncomfortable speak of this."

He sighed. Then, very lightly, he touched her shoulder. "That's all right, Mrs. Fujimoto. But if the police talk to you, you must tell them about this—understand? It could be important; it may relate to what *really* happened to that poor girl. You must tell them."

Nodding slowly, she said, "Yes, Mr. Burroughs. I understand. If police ask, I tell them."

"Good. Good."

Hully had come in shortly after that, and father and son had strolled to the beach and filled each other in on what they had learned so far, in their informal investigation.

At the game, Burroughs had watched the one-sided affair with only mild interest; and Wooch Fielder— casual in a short-sleeved blue aloha shirt and khaki trousers—applauded and occasionally cheered, but he too seemed distracted. Burroughs didn't mention the murder, waiting to see if the colonel would bring it up.

The halftime show was a binge of patriotism, a colorful, musical pageant that the crowd ate up. Fifteen marching bands—with a crack Marine unit in the lead—combined into one massive crew, playing island favorites like "Hawaii Ponoi," the inescapable Shriner anthem "I'm Forever Blowing Bubbles," and such flag-waving fare as "Stars and Stripes Forever." The lavish exhibition included a rare daylight array of fireworks, one of whose rockets delivered a miniature Hawaiian flag, followed by another that sent the American flag wafting down in a shower of sparks, though the unfurling barely occurred before it hit the ground, due to a slight malfunction. After all of his friend Teske's talk of Japanese invasion, Burroughs could not keep from wondering if the latter was a portent.

Also, the creator of Tarzan and John Carter of Mars could not keep from noticing white clouds piling up in the placid blue of the sky into what seemed to him the unmistakable formation of a monster, whose long tongue lashed side to side. Another omen? At times like these, Edgar Rice Burroughs could have done without his vivid imagination.

As the second half got under way, Burroughs finally looked over at his friend and said, "I'm a little surprised you haven't said anything about that girl's murder."

Fielder gave Burroughs a quick sideways look, then

said, as if commenting on the rising price of wheat, "Well, it's certainly a terrible thing."

"How's your son taking it?"

Now some humanity came into Fielder's hawkish face. "Very hard, I'm afraid. I don't even know where he is, he rushed off after we . . . He came looking for me. . . ."

Burroughs frowned. "Why would he come looking for you?"

Fielder was lighting up a cigarette. "He just needed to take it out on someone. . . . 'Are you satisfied?'. . . . That kind of thing. To be expected."

"Hully was the one who broke it to him. Hell of a thing."

With a sigh of smoke, Fielder said, "Poor Hully. . . . I hope he can help Bill. I'm afraid I won't be able to break through the resentment for some time."

Bill and Wooch had a somewhat strained relationship, anyway—that the boy had joined the Navy, rather than the Army, in an effort to step out from under his father's shadow, had been a point of contention. On the other hand, Burroughs believed that Fielder was secretly proud of his son, for taking that stand.

"Did you and Bill ever argue about the planned marriage?"

"Actually, yes—last night, after the luau, he came to see me . . . to state his case. I'm afraid I was rather rough on the boy. Nothing I can do about it now."

Burroughs studied his friend. "Pearl Harada came to see me, not long before she was killed—to ask if I'd arrange a meeting between the two of you."

Fielder gave Burroughs a sharp look. "Really? Whatever for?"

"Same thing, I suppose—make a case for the marriage. You didn't talk to her?"

"I never met the young woman. I'm sorry she's dead." The colonel shrugged. "That's the end of it."

"Jesus, Wooch—that's a little cold, isn't it?"

He exhaled smoke. "All I care about is the best for my boy—and marrying that girl would've been a tragedy."

"Her death's the tragedy, Wooch."

Fielder said nothing; he was watching the game.

Burroughs applauded as the Rainbows made another first down. "That fellow Morimura, that so-called diplomat, he was seen bawling out the Harada girl, a few hours before she was killed."

Another sharp, interested look. "Is that right? I wonder . . ."

"What, Wooch?"

"Well, possibly that little Jap was one of her lovers. She was something of a tart, I understood."

Burroughs blinked. "I wouldn't refer to her that way, to your son, if I were you."

Fielder turned toward the writer and some of the hardness seemed to melt. "Ed . . . I don't mean to be a bastard. I'm not unfeeling. But the very fact that this girl attracted a murderer . . . that some suitor of hers felt compelled to kill her, in some crime of passion . . . that makes *my* case, doesn't it? That Bill is better off without her."

Suddenly six-two Adam Sterling was pushing in next

to Burroughs, finally taking his seat. "Sorry I'm a little late."

"A little late?" Burroughs said. "It's the third quarter and your guys are behind fourteen and haven't made a dent on the scoreboard."

Sterling shrugged. "I'm afraid it is a lost cause for the Bearcats."

The FBI agent was in a white linen suit with a dark blue tie; he looked as if he'd just come from the office—which Burroughs figured was probably the case.

The score climbed to twenty to nothing, and Sterling didn't even appear to care; he, too, seemed distracted, terribly so. The game he'd been looking forward to, so eagerly, suddenly seemed to mean nothing.

Finally Sterling leaned across Burroughs and whispered to Fielder, "What are your plans, after the game?"

"My wife and I are going to a party tonight, at Schofield Barracks—with General Short and his wife."

"Something's come up I need to fill you in on, Colonel—really need to see what you make of it."

Sterling clearly meant business, his handsome, bronzed features fist-tight, his voice knife-edged. And Fielder, after all, was chief of Army intelligence on Oahu. . . .

Fielder, eyes narrowed, obviously reading this, said, "I don't think your team's going to come back—shall we go somewhere and talk?"

"You going to leave me here?" Burroughs asked. "To endure this one-sided contest alone?"

Sterling looked at Burroughs, then at Fielder. "I think Ed can hear this."

Fielder shrugged. "It's your call."

Within twenty minutes, the trio was seated in a thatched-roof pergola on the stretch of beach that belonged to the Waikiki Tavern, which despite its saloon-style name was perhaps Honolulu's most cosmopolitan restaurant. The beachfront arbor was theirs alone, giving the three men both privacy and a breathtaking view of Diamond Head, that distinctive extinct crater whose green slopes danced with sunlight and shadows.

Fielder and Sterling had ordered rum punches and Burroughs was drinking iced tea. The FBI agent had explained to Fielder that Burroughs was doing a little informal surveillance work at the Niumalu and that Burroughs (revealing a fact of which the writer was previously unaware) had been given a security clearance by J. Edgar Hoover himself, for that very purpose.

Sterling got a notebook out of the inside pocket of his white linen jacket, saying, "I went in to the office this morning because of several disturbing events. One was the murder of Pearl Harada."

Fielder frowned skeptically. "How would a girl singer's murder have an impact on intelligence?"

"I can't imagine," Sterling admitted. "But the supposed eyewitness to her murder, Otto Kuhn, is believed to be a 'sleeper' agent for Japan. Kuhn lives at the Niumalu, you know—he's the character Ed is helping keep an eye on."

Fielder nodded, lighting up a cigarette. "You said 'several' disturbing events—what else?"

The colonel did not seem keen to discuss the Pearl Harada killing.

The FBI agent leaned forward. "We've learned that the Japanese Consulate has spent much of the week disposing of—burning—its papers. Considering the present situation, that would seem goddamn significant—a definite indication that the end of peaceful relations between our two nations is close at hand."

"Everyone knows we're heading for war with Japan," Fielder said, sighing smoke, not seeming terribly impressed. "It doesn't surprise me that they're cleaning house. What else?"

"Well, as you know," Sterling said, shifting in his wicker chair, "we record every radiophone call made between here and Tokyo."

"That's been a matter of routine for months," Fielder said, apparently for Burroughs's benefit.

"When I came in to the office this morning, with these other matters on my mind, I was presented with a transcript translation of a radiophone conversation. Seems yesterday afternoon, a reporter at a Tokyo newspaper placed a call to Honolulu." Sterling referred to the little notebook. "His name is Ogawa, and his paper is the *Yomiuri Shinbun*."

Fielder sipped his rum punch.

"The call was to Mrs. Ishiko Mori," Sterling elaborated, "a Japanese citizen living here, married to a prominent *nisei* dentist."

"Why is a Tokyo paper interviewing a dentist's wife?" Fielder asked.

"Mrs. Mori is a journalist—a stringer for the paper. She'd been asked to round up prominent members of the Japanese-American community for interviews— some kind of feature on everyday life in Honolulu. But Mrs. Mori reported to Ogawa that no one wanted to participate; possibly with the current state of relations between Japan and America, the idea made them . . . nervous. So Mrs. Mori answered the questions herself."

"What sort of questions?"

"Whether airplanes were flying daily, and were they 'big' planes . . . the latter could be significant, because that would indicate long-range recon missions. Most of the questions Ogawa asked had to do with Oahu's defenses."

"Such as?"

"Such as whether the fleet was in . . . were there searchlights on the planes flying at night . . . that kind of thing."

Fielder said, "That's information available to anybody in the city."

"Legal spying?" Burroughs asked. "Like the snooping that Morimura character's been up to?"

Sterling seemed a bit surprised at Burroughs knowing this, and though the writer had intended his words for Fielder, the FBI agent answered: "Exactly like that. But one exchange between the reporter and the dentist's wife really caught my attention."

Again Sterling referred to the notebook.

" 'What kind of flowers are in bloom in Hawaii at

present?' Ogawa asked her," the FBI agent reported. "And Mrs. Mori said, 'The hibiscus and poinsettias are in bloom now.' "

Fielder seemed almost amused. "And, what? You believe this to be code?"

"I believe she may have been reporting on the movement of specific battleships, yes."

Burroughs, knowing he was out of his element, had largely kept mum; but now he couldn't resist, saying, "Wooch, if somebody in Tokyo did invent this flower code, and was willing to spend upwards of two hundred bucks for a fifteen-minute transpacific call . . . could Frank Teske have been right? Are we in imminent danger of air attack?"

Fielder ignored Burroughs, saying to Sterling, "Do you have the full transcript with you?"

Sterling said, "Yes," eagerly withdrawing the several folded sheets from his jacket pocket. He handed them to Fielder, who sat and read them, while Sterling and Burroughs waited. The pergola was so near the water, the view of the surf and its riders was particularly peaceful; the silhouette of Diamond Head seemed so tranquil, the concerns the FBI man had been expressing were absurd in contrast.

But Burroughs had seen a dead girl on these white sands, the night before, and was inclined to pay attention.

The chief of Army intelligence, however, was not overawed. Handing the transcript back, Fielder said, "It seems like quite an ordinary message. Sounds like just the sort of mundane stuff a newspaperman would need for a feature story on life in present-day Honolulu."

"Colonel," Sterling said, "I can't agree—I know nothing here can be clearly defined as manifestly dangerous to security . . . but the general tone of the conversation, in light of suspicious activity by a German 'sleeper' agent, and the Jap Consulate burning their papers . . . Wooch, damnit, man—I have a sick feeling about this."

Fielder crushed his cigarette out in a little metal ashtray. He was nodding. "Fair enough. I'll tell General Short you want an appointment, Monday morning."

"No—tonight. As soon as possible."

The colonel looked up, sharply. "I told you, Adam— the general has plans for the evening."

"Then I'll meet with him on his goddamn front porch. I have to insist, Colonel. These Moris are on my list of potentially disloyal Japs. I'm positive this call means something—something's definitely in the wind."

Fielder sighed heavily. He finished off his rum punch and said, "All right, you stubborn s.o.b. Can you meet me at my quarters at six o'clock?"

"Yes. Absolutely."

Nodding, Fielder rose; the two men shook hands. "See you there."

And Colonel Fielder headed toward the tavern and its parking lot.

"I think you're doing the right thing," Burroughs said.

"Hell," Sterling said with a laugh. The FBI man gulped down the rest of his rum punch. "I was just hoping I was full of crap."

# NINE

## *Chinatown*

For a Coast *haole* (as mainlanders were referred to), Hully Burroughs had a better-than-average understanding of Hawaii's Japanese community.

He knew that Japanese owned many of the restaurants in Honolulu, that they repaired most cars and built most houses, that they worked behind most retail counters. And, anyway, you didn't have to be terribly aware to notice the dozens of Japanese teahouses, or the kimono shops, or the sake breweries, the Japanese-language newspapers, fish-cake factories, movie houses. . . .

Still, much of this eluded the average *haole,* particularly the typical tourist, because on the one hand, Hawaii worked hard at its Polynesian image—Waikiki wallowed in it—and on the other, Hawaii was insistent upon its American status, indignantly reminding forgetful mainlanders that they were in the United States, not some foreign land.

Hully had gained his awareness, limited though it might be, through his friendship with Sam Fujimoto, the son of their maid at the Niumalu. Sam—a senior in prelaw at the University of Hawaii—had shown Hully the local ropes, when the mainlander had first arrived.

This afternoon, Hully needed his friend's help, for two reasons. First, he needed wheels—his father had taken the Pierce Arrow to the Shriner game. Second, he needed a tour guide—because, despite whatever scant familiarity he had with local Asian customs, Hully felt that would not be enough for where he needed to go.

Chinatown. The Oriental neighborhood had been staked out many decades before by Chinese workers fleeing the sugar and pineapple plantations, marking off this triangle of downtown Honolulu—Nuuanu Street on the southeast, North Beretania Street on the northeast, South King Street as the hypotenuse—for small retail businesses and restaurants.

But despite the name, in Chinatown, the Japanese (and the Filipinos, too, for that matter) vastly outnumbered the Chinese, though the white tourists, coming and going from the main port at the foot of Nuuanu Street, rarely knew the difference, much less noticed how the Japanese and Chinese merchants kept their distance from each other, even when jammed side by side.

Coast *haoles* saw only the Orient, a nonspecific Asia crammed into a few blocks—sleazy storefronts and Shinto shrines, silk shops and tattoo parlors, bathhouses and Buddhist temples, live chickens and dead ducks, coffee shops and chop suey joints, incense and strangely aromatic spices mingling with the sickly-sweet perfume of the nearby pineapple canneries and the salty stench of the marshlands below the city.

"What do you think her uncle's likely to know?" Sam Fujimoto asked.

The slender, smoothly handsome *nisei*—black hair trimmed military short (he was in ROTC at the Manoa campus)—was casual at the wheel of his dark blue '38 Ford convertible sedan; his sportshirt was a lighter blue, his trousers white, his shoes the slippers so common on the island (Hully was wearing a pair himself).

"You and I, we only knew Pearl through the Niumalu," Hully said. "The only people in her life that we know, too, are musicians, hotel staff and guests."

"And boyfriends like Bill and that Stanton character, who met her there."

"Right, Sam. But she used to live with her uncle, in Chinatown, when she first moved to Oahu—that could open up a whole new world of friends and acquaintances."

"Maybe it is worth talking to him." Sam had never dated Pearl, but he knew her a little, had spoken to her a few times. "But it'll probably be a dead end. My feeling is, she distanced herself from anything ... overtly Japanese." He shrugged. "A lot of my generation do."

"Pearl sure seemed like an all-American girl."

One hand on the wheel, Sam gave Hully half a smile. "She *was* one—she was born in Frisco, right?"

"Right."

The convertible was bouncing along Fort Street. They crossed Nuuanu Street, where the Liberty Theater—home to a Chinese stock company that went in for horrific flights of fancy—was at the left.

"I think I've seen this guy around the Niumalu," Sam said, referring to Yoshio Harada, Pearl's grocer uncle. Though he didn't live at the hotel, Sam had spent his share of time there, what with his mother's work and his friendship with Hully.

"I saw him just yesterday," Hully said. "Helped him unload, a little. Bivens buys fresh seafood and fruit and vegetables from Harada. Seems like a nice enough little guy . . . You would think he'd be heartsick, today."

"His niece murdered, I should say."

Actually, Hully had his doubts, though he said, "Maybe he won't even be working."

"Oh, he'll be working," Sam said with a knowing smile. "Guy like that doesn't miss a Saturday at the market."

Hully knew Sam was right—knew that Harada was indeed working today. Since Hully hadn't had an address for the grocer, he'd stopped at the front desk and checked with manager Fred Bivens, who'd said, "Funny thing is, you just missed him. He made a delivery not ten minutes ago."

"Really? Gosh, he delivered a boatload of stuff just yesterday—I helped him unload some of it."

"I remember—but sometimes Mr. Harada makes unscheduled stops when he has something nice for me—like the swordfish he dropped by with, just now."

"How's he doing?"

"Doing?"

"His niece was murdered last night, Fred. How is he doing?"

"Oh. Well, he's doing fine. I paid my sympathies, he thanked me, we both said what a sad awful thing it was, and . . . frankly, then we did business."

"So Pearl's uncle isn't holed up in some funeral home or church, mourning, then."

"No. He said he was on his way back to his store."

"You have an address?"

"Actually . . . funny thing, no. I never been down there to his shop in Chinatown . . . he always makes deliveries. All I know is it's down near the Aala Market."

They were deep into Chinatown now. Just past Maunakea Street, on the right-hand side of Beretania, was notorious Tin Can Alley, that quaint, exotic, harmless-looking entry into a deadly tenement area replete with crooked pathways, whores, rickety wooden stairs, pimps, sagging balconies, and thugs—a literal tourist trap. Within easy walking distance were neighborhoods with such sobriquets as Blood Town, Hell's Half Acre and Mosquito Flats, home to a staggering array of opium dens, gambling halls and cathouses.

"What's your take on this?" Hully asked his friend. "You know Bill well enough—could he be a suspect?"

Sam shrugged a shoulder. "Only if Pearl was running around on him, and he caught her in the act."

"Do you believe that's possible?"

"She was a flirt, and she got around—but this last month or so? I can't see it. Hell, she was crazy about

Bill—she was serious. They were serious."

Nodding thoughtfully, Hully said, "I'd like to track down this Stanton—he's on a weekend pass. Maybe we could check out Hotel Street later."

"I'm game."

Just beyond Lau Yee Chai—the best, most lavish chop suey house in Honolulu (a different sort of tourist trap)—was River Street, bordering the Nuuanu Stream. Soon they were on Queen Street, and Sam found a parking place, and they headed over on foot to the Aala Market and the Japanese sampan fishing dock.

Along the way they encountered Japanese women wearing silk kimonos clip-clopping along the wooden walkway in clogs called *gettas,* lugging children on their backs. Past the garish Oriental lettering of signs, small simple wooden storefronts were gorged with tourist-friendly merchandise; often a diapered baby would be crawling across a wooden floor, and one moonfaced older child sat unattended, nibbling pink gelatin candies, while tourists and clerks bartered. They passed pawnshops, *saimin* (noodle) cafés, coffee shops, and herb dens, the babblelike sounds of Asian tongues mingling with the occasional popping of firecrackers and the hollow echo of gongs gliding down the Nuuanu Valley from a Buddhist temple.

The Aala Market was democracy—and capitalism—in action: all classes of people, half a dozen or more races, moving along the vegetable, fish and flower stalls, rubbing (sometimes knocking) elbows in the common pursuit of food. The fish caught in Hawaiian waters were second to none, and spread out in rows for the approval of customers: red snappers looking like giant goldfish; enormous swordfish; tuna small and large (*aku*); bass; needlefish; even an octopus. Some of it had been chopped into slabs and steaks, and there was seaweed for sale, too, and dried salmon, and fresh *poi*.

Hully let Sam do the talking—since much of it was in Japanese—seeking directions to the grocer's shop. Sam had little luck for some time, until Hully thought to ask him to explain to these merchants that they were not seeking Harada to make a purchase.

"I should've thought of that," Sam said, grinning, shaking his head. "They don't want to send us to a competitor!"

Next time out, they got the address—and it was close by.

As they strolled along the sampan dock, where both small blue sampans and larger diesel-powered boats were moored, Sam said, "These fishermen are all Japanese—no Chinese or Filipino or anybody else."

"Why?"

"We're just better at it." This was a rare instance of Sam referring to himself as in any way Japanese. "Faster boats, powerful shortwave radios. We're good at gizmos."

"Size of some of these boats is amazing."

"Fishing is big business, around here—one of those diesel-powered forty-footers can run you twelve grand. That kind of dough even Tarzan wouldn't sneeze at."

Hully whistled. "You know, all this talk of a Japanese attack on Oahu—would they really do it? I mean, there are so many Japanese here . . . so much Japanese business."

"Well, it's really American business, Hully. But you have a point—Honolulu is probably the most Japanese city on earth, outside Japan."

"So you're saying they wouldn't bomb us?"

"No." And Sam's eyes tightened into slits, and his smile was utterly mirthless. "They'd bomb us in a flash."

"That's hard for me to believe."

Sam put a hand on his friend's shoulder. "Hully, there are quite likely people in Japan right now banking on that very attitude."

Yoshio Harada's shop was not a grocery in any American sense. It was a small, unpretentious wooden storefront whose front door was black hanging beads; the walls were consumed with shelves overflowing with reed baskets and glass jars of ginger root, shark-fins, seahorse skeletons, dried seaweed and other exotic wares. None of the fresh fish or produce that Harada delivered to the Niumalu (and, presumably, other clients) was on display—apparently, he strictly made his purchases at the nearby Aala Market for deliveries by pick-up truck.

The small, mustached man—wearing a white shirt and tan trousers and a grocer's apron, despite the lack of groceries—was manning a counter to the left, the shelves of weird roots and herbs rising surrealistically behind him.

Harada recognized Hully at once, half-bowing. "Ah,

Burroughs-san. You honor me. What brings you to Chinatown?"

"I came to pay my respects." Hully gestured to Sam. "This is my friend Sam Fujimoto—his mother is our maid at the Niumalu—perhaps you know her."

"I am sorry, I do not. But it is a pleasure." Harada held out his hand and he and Sam shook, like they were both Americans . . . which, of course, they were.

"I was a friend of your niece's, as well, sir," Sam said, with another respectful nod. "We're sorry for your loss."

The grocer offered a curt nod in return. "Thank you, gentlemen."

"When will the service be held?" Hully asked.

Harada seemed confused. "Service?"

"Pearl's funeral."

"Oh . . . no arrangements have been made."

"Ah. Can I help?"

"I have written her parents. Posted the letter."

"You didn't call them?"

"No. It is long distance."

Hully exchanged glances with Sam. "But Mr. Harada, surely Pearl deserves better than this. . . . As I said, I'll be glad to help. . . ."

"Offer is . . . kind." Harada smiled faintly, patiently. "Burroughs-*san,* I like my niece, but we were not . . . close. I am Buddhist, she was Christian. She would not want a service in my faith; I no have interest in arranging one in hers. Her parents share her Christian belief. They may feel other way."

Frowning, Hully asked, "Where is her body now?"

"I understand is in morgue. She was murdered."

"Well, I know she was murdered, but—"

Harada held up a hand. His face was strangely hard. "I am sorry for her death. But she turned her back on her people. She did not like it here, with me—and she did not return, once she got her . . . job."

"I thought she helped line you up your grocery account with Fred Bivens, at the Niumalu."

"She did. I was grateful."

Sam said, "But you weren't close."

"No."

Hully tried another angle. "Did she have any friends down here? Or for that matter, enemies?"

Harada's eyes narrowed; his face seemed to harden even more. "Why do you ask this?"

"Well, someone killed her. . . ."

Harada's chin lifted. "A man is under arrest. She had loose morals and a man killed her. He is in custody, is he not?"

"Yeah, sure, but—"

"The circle has closed. Why do you ask questions as if you are a policeman?"

Hully gestured with an open hand. "Mr. Harada, I meant no offense. I merely . . . we merely . . . thought we'd offer our sympathies in what we had assumed would be a dark hour, for you."

Harada said nothing.

Sam said, "I guess that was our mistake."

For several long seconds, Hully just stared at the little grocer, who didn't even blink. Then Hully rushed out onto the wooden sidewalk, anger bubbling; Sam followed.

Hully was several storefronts down, moving quickly through the interracial crowd, when Sam caught up with him. "Take it easy, Hul. . . . You just ran head-on into a cultural war I've fought every day of my life."

Hully stopped, looked at his friend. "Something smells."

"Yeah, fish and dirty diapers and incense. What, you think Harada killed his own niece? Why? Because she was Christian?"

Hully didn't know what to say, and was still looking for words when a small dark man in a snap-brim fedora, orange tie, and brown rumpled suit was suddenly in their midst.

"What the hell do you think you're doing?" Detective John Jardine demanded. His dark eyes were daggers.

"I, uh . . . well . . ."

Jardine took Hully by the back of the arm and hustled him into a booth in a nearby café. Sam came along, a wide-eyed bystander, who slipped in next to Hully.

A waitress in a kimono came over, and Jardine said, "Three coffees," and she went away.

"You were grilling that guy," Jardine said.

"You . . . you heard?"

"There's no damn door. Sure I heard—I was on my way in to interrogate him myself. What in the hell are you doing, walking my damn beat?"

Calmly, Hully said, "Have you talked to my dad today?"

"No—we've missed each other, traded phone calls. Why, is he in this too?"

With another glance at Sam, who shrugged, Hully sighed and made a clean breast it—sharing not only the notion of the informal investigation he and his father had been conducting, but the various pieces of information they had discovered.

Though he looked irritated, the Portuguese detective jotted much of this down in his small notebook.

"Thank you for the information," Jardine said, sliding the notebook into an inside suit-jacket pocket. "Now—give your father a message for me: leave this to the professionals. I won't write about his jungle, and you and your father need to stay the hell out of mine."

Hully leaned forward. "Are you looking at any suspects, other than Harry Kamana?"

An eyebrow arched. "I was about to interview that grocer, wasn't I? Damnit, boy—leave this to the police." He looked sharply at Sam. "What's your part in this?"

Sam's eyes widened. "I'm just a friend of Hully's . . . I was a friend of Pearl's, too."

"Where were you last night?"

"At a college dance—pregame bash."

"But you weren't at the game today?"

"I don't like football."

"But you went to the 'pregame bash'?"

"Well, sure—I do like girls."

"Did you like Pearl Harada?"

"Not that way . . . hey, what is this?"

Jardine looked pointedly at Hully. "How's this guy

for another suspect? We're looking at everybody and everything . . . including you, Mr. Burroughs."

A uniformed officer, a young Polynesian, peered in the café's storefront window and seemed relieved to see Jardine. The cop hurried in and stood next to the booth, hands behind him.

"Detective, may I have a word?"

Jardine rose and, pointing to Hully and then at Sam, said, "Stay," as if to a pair of dogs.

Hully and Sam watched out the window as the uniformed cop delivered some slice of detailed information that made Jardine cover his mouth; then the detective pushed his fedora back on his head, and turned and gazed through the café window at Hully. He crooked a finger.

Hully raised his eyebrows and gestured to himself.

Jardine frowned and nodded.

Soon Sam had been left behind and Jardine—with the uniformed cop at the wheel—was sitting in the front seat of a squad car with Hully in back, feeling like a suspect.

"What's this about?" Hully asked.

"Just ride," Jardine said.

Past the end of the Waikiki streetcar line, Jardine's driver headed out Diamond Head Road. The road was just about to begin making its winding way up the cliffs, when the squad car drew up along the roadside where another squad car was already parked.

Wordlessly, Jardine approached an opening between the rocks where another Polynesian uniformed cop was posted at the mouth of the path; the cop nodded to

Jardine and pointed down. Following the swarthy little detective—whose driver had stayed behind—Hully did his best to keep his balance as he navigated vari-sized rocks down the grassy, sandy slope. On the beach below, the rock-infested white beach, lay a body—a naked man, sprawled on his stomach. Two more cops stood watch, but this fellow wasn't going anywhere.

The sand was moist under his slippers, as Hully trailed after the detective, who made a beeline to the body and knelt. The nude, slender frame of the corpse became a specific person when Hully got close enough to see the pale, sand-flecked, bulging-eyed face, the surf rolling up nearby, threatening to dampen the dead features.

"Recognize him?" Jardine said to Hully, looking up from beside the body.

"Terry Mizuha," Hully said. His tongue felt thick; his head was spinning. He turned away from the corpse, walked a few steps down the beach, his back to the cops and the body.

Then Jardine was at his side. "You said this boy might have more information to share."

Hully had included a summary of his conversation with the (late) guitar player when he had filled Jardine in, at the Chinatown coffee shop.

"Yes—he said he had to think . . . to 'sort things out.' He'd said maybe we'd talk in a few hours."

"It's been a few hours—but Terry doesn't seem too talkative."

Hully swallowed, shivered. "How was he killed?"

The wind off the ocean was threatening to whip

away Jardine's fedora, but somehow it stayed put. "Garroted—probably with a small rope."

Hully shook his head—such a violent way for so gentle a soul to meet his fate. "Do you still think Harry Kamana killed Pearl Harada?"

Jardine twitched a nonsmile. "I'd say a little doubt is raised."

Hully snorted a humorless laugh. "Well, Kamana sure as hell didn't kill this guy! I saw Terry at the Niumalu, well before lunch!"

Jardine heaved a sigh, and looked back toward the body. "We were probably not meant to find him so soon. . . . This is a rocky portion of the beach, not visible from the highway. But some tourists stumbled across him . . . forty-five minutes ago."

"What's the significance of finding him sooner, rather than later?"

The sharp eyes landed back on Hully; the faintest of smiles etched itself on Jardine's thin lips. "I'm supposed to write this off as a *mahu* kill."

"A what?"

"*Mahu* . . . fairy—homosexual. Lots of queers get killed in Waikiki, usually by soldiers or sailors. Kind of a . . . local tradition that horny servicemen, short of money, pick up a *mahu* on a street corner for a free 'thrill.' Some of these servicemen are sickened by the experience, and take it out on the poor bastards, after."

"You don't really think this is a—"

"No. But I'm supposed to. Terry Mizuha was a known *mahu*—and he's nude, possibly preparing for . . . you know."

"In the middle of the day?"

Jardine frowned. "That's why I say we weren't supposed to find him so soon. . . . I would like to talk to your servicemen friends, Fielder and Stanton."

"Why, you think one of them may have lured him out here, on a pretext?"

"Possibly. It's secluded enough, even for a daytime tryst. Anyway, there are no signs of the body being carried down the slope. He would seem to have been killed here, on the beach."

"But he *could* have been killed elsewhere."

"Yes—if the killer had an accomplice to help him carry the body down the slope. The body could have been transported here in the trunk of a car."

"Did you find the clothes?"

Jardine nodded. "I'm told they were neatly stacked in the rocks nearby."

The afternoon was dying. The setting sun seemed a red-hot ball of flame, tinting the waves pink, as if the ocean were watered-down blood.

The detective looked up at Hully with eyes that were bright but no longer hard or sharp. "Would you help me tonight, Mr. Burroughs? We'll go to Hotel Street and find that sailor and that soldier."

There was no question about it: Hully would go along with Jardine. But just the same, he said, "I thought I was supposed to leave this to the professionals."

"You'll be with a professional. What do you say?"

Down the beach, foamy surf licking ever nearer, Terry Mizuha seemed to have no objection.

"I had nothing else planned," Hully said.

# TEN

## *An Evening at the Shuncho-ro*

At the top of Red Hill, Burroughs slowed his Pierce Arrow to take in the panoramic view of Pearl Harbor on this peaceful evening—the scattering of stars in God's purple Hawaiian sky competing with the man-made twinkling of buildings and ships, the ebony sea highlighted shimmeringly by the rays of the near-golden moon. Dance band music drifted up from the officers' club below, the view including the Naval Station, Luke Field, and—in the distance—the Ewa Sugar Plantation; but the equipment, the trappings, of the great base were lost in the night, the workshops, the big hammerhead crane, swallowed by darkness, with only the lights of the Pacific Fleet remaining—and there were plenty, what with every battleship in port.

Winding down the hill, passing through Halawa Gulch, the convertible glided by fields of sugarcane, which waved at the writer, friendly in the moonlight.

A sign told Burroughs that Pearl City Road Junction lay ahead just three miles, where a left turn would take him to the Peninsula residential section and the Shuncho-ro teahouse.

He had not connected with Hully, and Burroughs wondered what his son might have uncovered—he only hoped the boy hadn't gotten himself in any jam. For once Burroughs valued his son's friendship with Sam Fujimoto—snooping in Chinatown without a safari guide would have been reckless. Not that he was worried, really, other than a standard fatherly concern: Hully was as smart as he was strapping, and could damn well take care of himself.

On the other hand, it *was* a murderer they were chasing. And Burroughs was starting to wonder whether Pearl Harada's death really had been a simple crime of passion, driven by the jealousy of one suitor or another . . . or was it a small yet important part of something greater and far more sinister?

Back at the Waikiki Tavern, after Colonel Fielder had departed, Burroughs and FBI agent Sterling had sat and talked for another fifteen minutes, in the thatched-roofed pergola on the beach. No more rum punch: a waiter was dispatched to bring coffee for both men. As they spoke, a tropical sunset painted the water, the world, with shades of red and orange; but as the sun's ball of fire slipped over the horizon, darkness rapidly invaded.

Burroughs had told Sterling about the informal investigation he and his son were undertaking into the Harada girl's death, assuring the agent that Hully had not been clued in on Otto Kuhn's suspected status as a sleeper agent.

"To me, the most interesting thing you've come up with," the ruggedly handsome FBI agent said, stirring sugar into his coffee, "is that phone call that Kuhn and his wife argued about."

Burroughs lifted an eyebrow. "Apparently Otto told her to deny there'd been any phone call, or anyway not to mention there had been one."

Sterling's eyes narrowed. "But who rang Otto, in the middle of the night? And why?"

"He's a sleeper agent—maybe it was a wake-up call."

The FBI agent nodded. "Maybe in a way it was— Otto receives a call, and then before you know it, he's on your doorstep, telling Jardine he witnessed Kamana killing that girl."

"You mean . . . the real murderer called him, and ordered up an alibi?"

Sterling made an openhanded shrugging gesture. "There's really only two reasonable alternatives, here: Kuhn did the killing and blamed Kamana; or someone else did the killing, and Kuhn is alibiing for him . . . or her."

"Her? Mrs. Kuhn, you mean?"

"She remains a viable suspect," Sterling said, and sipped his coffee. "Otto's reputation as a playboy has been well earned—he does run around on Elfriede . . . and you gotta give Otto his nerve for that: his wife is the niece of Heinrich Himmler himself."

The saltwater breeze suddenly seemed chilly to Burroughs. "So I really do have Nazis living next door."

"No doubt of that."

"Then where does the damn phone call come in?"

Sterling threw his hands up. "Search me. But I can tell you this—there's a reason why Pearl Harada's murder sent up a warning flare at my office . . . particularly with Otto Kuhn as a supposed eyewitness, apparently fingering a fall guy."

"Why is that, Adam?"

The agent leaned forward. "Remember what I told you about the network of *nisei* who are helping compile a list of potentially disloyal Japs here in Oahu?"

"Sure."

"Well, Pearl Harada's uncle—the Chinatown grocer—is on that list."

Burroughs half climbed out of his wicker chair. "Jesus, Hully went to question that guy this afternoon!"

Sterling patted the air, calmingly. "I didn't say Uncle Harada was dangerous—just that he's loyal to his native country . . . like a lot of *issei* in Chinatown."

*Issei* were first-generation immigrants.

Sterling was saying, "Until recently, Harada displayed photographs of the emperor in his shop. Plus, he's vocally supported Japan's war on China, buying Jap war bonds, helping organize an effort to send 'comfort bags' to Japanese soldiers—blankets, shoes, candy."

Burroughs shifted in his chair. "Well, this is beginning to look like Pearl Harada's death may have more to do with espionage than affairs of the heart."

Sterling shrugged again. "There's no question this

was a beautiful girl who could have driven a man to some irrational, jealous act of violence . . . but with both her uncle and your 'Nazi-next-door' in the scenario, an espionage-related motive remains a distinct possibility."

"And let's not forget she knew Vice Consul Morimura, either—or that he was reading her the Riot Act in the parking lot, a few hours before she was killed."

Sterling's reaction was not what Burroughs had expected: the FBI agent laughed.

Astounded, Burroughs said, "This is funny, all of a sudden?"

"I'm sorry. It's just . . . That guy's hard to take seriously. My guess is Morimura was yelling at her because she wouldn't give him the time of day."

"How can you say that, Adam? Fielder admits this clown spends most of his time engaged in 'legal' spying."

" 'Clown' is the key word, there." Sterling sipped his coffee, then leaned forward again. "Listen, Ed— Morimura is an idiot. I have it on good authority that everybody else at the Consulate hates his guts, considers him a lazy ass. We've had him under surveillance, from time to time, and the guy just wanders around like a tourist, never takes a note or a photo or makes a sketch."

"Maybe he has a photographic memory."

"I sincerely doubt it, considering all the brain cells he's lost to sake. Morimura's a simpleton and a sybarite."

Burroughs was shaking his head, astounded by

Sterling's attitude. "Kuhn's a playboy and you take *him* seriously."

"Morimura spends all his time drinking himself into a stupor and screwing geisha girls—end of story."

"Maybe he's just a clever agent—you were concerned enough about the Consulate burning their papers, yesterday, and Morimura's a damn vice consul. . . ."

Sterling held up his hands as if in surrender. "Check him out yourself, if you like, Ed—this is Saturday . . . he'll no doubt be at the Shuncho-ro teahouse, tonight. The management keeps a room upstairs for him, to pursue his debaucheries, and then sleep it off." Sterling checked his watch. "As for me, I have to get over to General Short's quarters, to try to jump-start him into taking all of these matters seriously . . . the Mori code, the Harada murder, the Consulate burning those papers. . . ."

Burroughs sighed, shook his head. "What the hell does it all mean, Adam?"

Sterling rose from his wicker chair. "Figuring that out isn't my job—my job is convincing General Short to figure it out."

The Shuncho-ro—Spring Tide Restaurant—was on Makanani Drive on the slopes of Alewa Heights, a surprisingly un-Oriental-looking two-story wooden house with generous picture windows on both floors and clean modern lines that wouldn't have been out of place back in Frank Lloyd Wright's Oak Park, Illinois, where Burroughs had lived in the teens. In the midst of a lush garden—no palms in sight—hugged by flow-

ering hedges, the Shuncho-ro perched on the moun-
tainside looking down on Honolulu, a breathtaking
view any tourist—or spy—might relish.

Burroughs left his Pierce Arrow in the dimly illu-
minated crushed-coral parking lot, which was fairly
full, the restaurant doing a good business. He noted,
parked on the other side of the lot, a black Lincoln
with a Japanese chauffeur in full livery asleep behind
the wheel—the vice consul's car, no doubt.

The writer also recognized another car in the lot, a
dark blue '41 Cadillac convertible. He'd seen this distinctive vehicle at the Niumalu many times: it belonged
to Otto Kuhn.

The wide entryway of the teahouse had horizontal
wooden spindlework on either side, a motif repeated in
the vestibule, a strong, stark design that again recalled
Oak Park's Frank Lloyd Wright—and Wright's own
Japanese inspiration. A host in a black suit and tie
asked if Burroughs had a reservation, which he did,
having called ahead; after leaving his shoes at the door,
Burroughs was shown by a teahouse girl in a pale blue
kimono to a low table for one, where he sat on a *tatami*
mat.

The sparsely decorated, oak-trimmed, cream-colored
dining room seemed about evenly divided between
Japanese-Americans and tourists, all of whom—like
Burroughs—were rather informally dressed, in
anticipation of the teahouse's sit-on-the-floor service.
He did not see Morimura or Kuhn among the diners
here on the first floor.

He drank a cup of tea, and when the geisha returned

for his order, he said, "I was hoping to link up with two friends of mine, who told me they'd be dining here, this evening—Otto Kuhn and Tadashi Morimura?"

She nodded. "The gentlemen are upstairs, sir."

"Wonderful! Which room?"

"Ichigo room—sign on door. It is private. May I announce you?"

Smiling, Burroughs got up. "No, that's all right— I'd rather surprise them. Can you direct me?"

The geisha was obliging—these girls were paid to be—and Burroughs was about to go up a stairway when he glimpsed somebody starting down. Ducking back around, tucking into the recess of the restroom hallway, Burroughs allowed Otto Kuhn to exit the stairwell and head out the entryway to the parking lot.

Then the writer slipped his shoes back on and followed after.

Kuhn moved quickly, his white linen suit flashing in the night, like a ghost on the run; but Burroughs trotted after him and caught up with the German near the parked Caddy.

"Well, Otto," Burroughs said, "we just keep bumping into each other."

Startled, Kuhn wheeled, blue eyes wide in the bland oval of his face. "Burroughs . . . Edgar. I didn't know you frequented the Shuncho-ro."

"My first time."

"You, uh, simply must try the *ogana* tonight . . . superb. Well, if you'll excuse me—"

Burroughs stopped him with a hand on an elbow.

"You're always in such a rush, Otto. I'm a driven, intense sort of fella myself . . . but I've learned to relax in Oahu."

Kuhn drew away from Burroughs's grasp. "Edgar, please, my wife is waiting."

"Really? You didn't take her along to the restaurant, on a Saturday night? I hope you two kids aren't having trouble."

Irritated, Kuhn frowned, saying, "She doesn't care for Japanese cuisine. If you'll *excuse* me . . ."

"Or maybe you were still doing business? I know you had business downtown, earlier—maybe this is an extension of that."

Kuhn's eyes hardened. "If it is business—it's *my* business . . . and, frankly, none of yours."

"Funny that you would be dining with Mr. Morimura, tonight, when you almost went out of your way, at the luau last night, to avoid him."

Mention of the vice consul's name had widened the blue eyes again; Kuhn had the look of a startled deer. "Who says I was dining with . . . what was the name?"

"Morimura, and the waitress in there said you and he had a private room upstairs."

Kuhn lifted his chin. "What are you implying?"

"Not romance. You see, Otto, I think somebody . . . maybe your Jap pal in there . . . called you last night, woke you and your lovely wife up."

"I don't know what you're talking about."

"I'm talking about you pinning a murder on that poor bastard Harry Kamana."

Kuhn's bland features contorted fiercely. "You're

out of your mind! I saw that musician bludgeon that girl with a rock—he bashed her damn skull in!"

"Did he? Or did you?"

The German drew back, sucking in a breath. Then, as if hurt, even offended, he said, "I don't have to put up with this."

"Maybe not from me . . . but my friend Detective Jardine, him you'll have to talk to. Last night you added to some already damning evidence to help make Kamana the obvious, and only, suspect. Today, though, things are looking different."

"What are you talking about?"

"I'm talking about that late-night phone call. I'm talking about your vice-consul pal in there bawling out that girl in public, just hours before her murder."

Kuhn shoved Burroughs, roughly, and the writer knocked into the next parked car with a metallic *whump*. Kuhn was opening his car door, getting in, when Burroughs latched onto his shoulder, spun him around and slammed a fist into his face.

His mouth bloody, Kuhn shoved Burroughs again, then went clawing inside his white jacket; the German's fingers were on a small black Lüger, snugged away in a shoulder holster, when Burroughs doubled him over with a hard fist to the belly.

Dazed, Kuhn tumbled to the crushed coral, sitting between his Caddy and the parked car next door, leaning on both hands, while Burroughs reached down and inside the man's jacket and plucked the Lüger like a hard little flower.

Then the writer pressed the automatic's barrel to the

German's forehead, and released the safety, a tiny click that echoed in the stillness of the night.

Eyes glittering with alarm, Kuhn said, "What do you want?"

"The truth. Did you see Kamana kill that girl?"

Swallowing thickly, the German shook his head, and the pressed-to-his-flesh pistol went along. "Morimura called me. Told me what to say."

"Did Morimura kill her?"

"I don't know. Maybe. I only know he wanted the musician identified. As far as I know, Kamana really could be the killer . . . I just . . . I just didn't see him do it."

"Why was Pearl Harada killed?"

"I don't know, I don't know. She flitted around— she was a pretty girl. Jealousy makes men crazy."

"Did you have an affair with her?"

"No! No. Of course not."

Burroughs pushed harder against the German's forehead. "What about Morimura?"

"I don't know! I don't know. . . . I'm not his goddamn chaperon."

"No, you're his stooge, though. Or should I say his understudy?"

Now the blue eyes tightened—alarm dissolving into fear. "Wh . . . what do you mean?"

"The Consulate's been busy burning its papers; coded messages to Japan have been flying. You're a good Nazi, aren't you, Otto? Waiting to help your ally, after we're at war, and diplomats like Morimura are suddenly prisoners. . . ."

Stiffly, Kuhn said, "I am not a Nazi."

"Should I pass that news along to your uncle Himmler?"

"Why are you . . . what are you . . . You're just a writer!"

"I'm just an American. Otto—did that girl's murder have anything to do with espionage?"

"What? No! How should I know?"

Burroughs pressed harder with the gun barrel. "Try again."

Trembling now, sweat pearling down his forehead, Kuhn said, "I swear to sweet Jesus I don't know. . . . I told you what you wanted! I admitted Morimura called me . . . that alone could get me killed."

Burroughs thought about that—then removed the gun from the German's forehead; it had left an impression, in several ways.

"Get the hell out of here," Burroughs told him, disgustedly.

Kuhn swallowed again. "What about my gun?"

"Spoils of war," Burroughs said, and dropped it into his pocket.

Kuhn didn't argue the point; he scrambled to his feet, climbed into his car and—as Burroughs headed back toward the Shuncho-ro—roared out, throwing crushed coral, finally waking up the Japanese chauffeur . . . for a few moments.

The word *Ichigo* appeared in both English and Japanese on a small oak plaque by an upstairs door. Burroughs knocked.

A male voice from within answered: "Yes?"

The writer spoke to the door. "Mr. Morimura? Ed Burroughs. Could I have a word with you?"

Moments later, the door cracked open. The handsome young Japanese diplomat stood eye to eye with Burroughs; Morimura's black hair was slicked back, and his slender form was wrapped up in an off-white robe with a scarlet sash. His feet were bare. He smelled heavily of musk.

"I do not understand, Mr. Burroughs." Morimura's expression was friendly but his dark eyes were not. "Why do you seek me here?"

Burroughs leaned a hand against the doorjamb. "I took a chance you might be at the Shuncho-ro. I heard it was kind of a second home to you."

"Could we not meet another time, another place?"

"This won't take long—I just want to chat for a few minutes. May I come in?"

"I have company."

Burroughs pushed the door open and shouldered past Morimura. At a low table, three Japanese girls wearing nothing at all were sitting on *tatami* mats. They were lovely of face and form, though their frozen embarrassment was painful to see.

"Put your kimonos on, girls," Burroughs said, "and take a break."

The pretty trio made sounds that mingled distress with giggling as they quickly got into their kimonos, which had been folded neatly on the floor behind them.

This was another sparsely decorated, oak-lined, cream-walled room; a row of big picture windows looked out onto the ocean . . . and Pearl Harbor, Ford

Island visible to the west, the Army's Hickam Field just to the left. A powerful telescope on a stand awaited any . . . tourist . . . who might want a better, closer look.

The now-clothed geishas scurried out past Morimura, who stood near the door with his arms folded, his face blank.

The consul said, "You are a rude and foolish man."

Burroughs strolled over and touched the telescope admiringly. "Maybe it's just cultural differences. Besides, I don't think *you're* a fool—even if everybody else seems to."

"Perhaps all Americans are foolish."

"They are if they don't think you're a damn spy."

Morimura smiled, almost gently. He gestured to the low table and the *tatami* mats. "Sake, Mr. Burroughs?"

"No thanks. I'm on the wagon."

"Wagon?"

"Never mind. But I'll sit with you, while you drink."

They sat across from each other at the low table; neither partook of the pitcher of sake.

Morimura's arms were again folded. "I am not a spy, Mr. Burroughs—I am a diplomat. Any information I have obtained has been through strictly legal means. Blame your own . . . American openness. Much can be gleaned from your daily newspapers, for example—and is there a law against looking through a telescope at a restaurant's lovely view?"

"Did you kill Pearl Harada?"

Morimura blinked, and his expression became one of horror. "What? What a ridiculous question!"

"Did you?"

"No. Certainly not. I barely knew her."

"Do you . . . 'barely' know her, the way you 'barely' know those three geisha girls?"

"No. The singer and I were not romantically involved."

"How about carnally?"

"No."

"Then why were you arguing with her, in the Niumalu parking lot, the night of her murder?"

Morimura's eyes widened—obviously, he didn't know he and Pearl had been seen.

"Her uncle asked me to speak to her."

"Her uncle? The grocer?"

"Yes. He heard rumors she was planning to marry an American boy. A sailor. He disapproved. I merely conveyed this message to her, and she was . . . disrespectful, both to me and in speaking of her uncle."

"Why didn't her uncle tell her this himself? He was around the Niumalu in the afternoon."

Morimura glared at Burroughs. "Why are you curious? What business is it to you, the murder of this girl?"

"I helped put the cuffs on Harry Kamana . . . I caught him at the beach with his hands bloody."

The diplomat nodded. "This I have heard."

"Between the two of us, you and me, we really nailed the poor bastard."

"The two of us? Nail? Your meaning escapes me."

"You called Otto Kuhn in the middle of the night, and had him pretend to be an eyewitness. You had him finger that musician."

"Nonsense."

"Kuhn told me himself."

Morimura frowned. "If so, he lies. When did he say this?"

"Just now, in the parking lot. I don't blame you for trading his company in on those geishas . . . no comparison. Anyway, Otto admitted you called him, and had him play eyewitness. You see, Otto receiving a call last night, well . . . that's a known fact."

"Really? I understood there was no switchboard at the Niumalu."

Burroughs grinned. "How interesting that you'd know a trivial detail like that, Mr. Morimura, considering you're not at all involved in this. By the way, don't take it out on Otto—he's afraid you'll kill him, or have him killed, because of what he told me."

"Did you bribe the German?"

"Hell no."

"Ah." Morimura's eyes narrowed. "I see the scrape on your knuckles. You beat it out of him." Morimura stood. "Perhaps you would care to try taking that . . . very American approach to seeking information . . . with me."

The consul moved away from the low table and struck a martial-arts pose. A single eyebrow raised, tiny smile on his thin lips, Morimura said, "Judo."

Burroughs rose and took the Lüger out and pointed it at him and said, "Gun."

Eyes flickering with fear, the supposed diplomat

slowly raised his hands. "Shoot me if you wish, Mr. Burroughs . . . but I will say nothing more. I am not like Otto Kuhn. I am not weak."

"And I'm not a murderer," Burroughs said, and slipped the gun in his pocket, and went out.

# ELEVEN

## *Hotel Street*

The exceptionally beautiful weather and the lopsided victory in this afternoon's football game coalesced into a night of rampant partying, excessive even for a Saturday in Honolulu. The city was rife with private parties and public revelry, and alive with music, from radios bleeding syrupy Hawaiian strains, seemingly designed to make lonely men feel even lonelier, to a lively battle of the bands at the Naval Receiving Station at Pearl Harbor, where the U.S.S. *Arizona* band was going over big, with the upbeat likes of "Take the A Train." Hotel ballrooms, like the Royal Hawaiian and the Ala Moana, were offering fox-trots, while swing music emanated from the town's less stodgy bandstands, like those at the Niumalu or the dance hall at Waikiki Amusement Park.

Swing also jumped from jukeboxes up and down Hotel Street, where sailors and soldiers swarmed in ribbons of white and khaki. A fleet of rickety taxis, wheezing buses and rattletrap jalopies charged down the two-lane highway connecting Pearl Harbor and Honolulu, conveying the invading horde to their dropping-off spot: the Army and Navy YMCA, at the eastern end of Hotel Street, a suitable starting point for an evening of good-natured debauchery.

Awash in garish neon, flickering under the strobe of fluorescent bulbs, Hotel Street was a glorified alleyway lined with low-slung stucco buildings wearing tin awnings like gambler's shades. To boys longing for home, the midway that was Hotel Street seemed to echo carnivals and state fairs, this rude collection of taverns, trinket counters, massage parlors, photo booths, pool halls, shooting galleries, curio stores, tattoo artists, and dime-a-dance joints.

Along the narrow sidewalks of every block were one or two barbershops, the barbers invariably young attractive Japanese women, and at least one lei shop, with pretty Hawaiian girls stringing flowers. Other sorts of "leis" were available, as well: hotels whose rooms all had the shades drawn—the Rex, the Anchor, the Ritz—attracted lines down the block of sailors and soldiers waiting to choose between two varieties of "room": three dollars for three minutes, or five dollars for an extended stay, up to ten. Relatively safe, too: the local police, in turning a blind if well-paid eye, insisted on weekly blood tests for these unofficially sanctioned soiled doves.

Hully and Jardine had recruited Sam Fujimoto to join on their Hotel Street expedition. Sam knew both

Ensign Bill Fielder and Corporal Jack Stanton, the former better than the latter, but in either case enough to
recognize either in this sea of uniforms. Starting at the
west end, Hully and Jardine, who were on a first-name
basis now, took one side of the street, while Sam took
the other—they had agreed to rendezvous at the Black
Cat Café in an hour and a half.

"You figure whoever killed Pearl Harada," Hully
said to the Portuguese detective, "killed Terry Mizuha,
as well."

They were shouldering their way down the tight,
teeming sidewalk, faces around them flushed with
neon—theirs, too.

"Probably," Jardine said.

"Why was Terry killed? What could he have
known?"

Jardine shrugged. "It's possible this Terry was a real
eyewitness . . . which may be more than can be said for
Otto Kuhn."

A group of sailors slouched under a tin awning in
front of a café, laughing, smoking, caps at jaunty an-
gles, pant legs flapping in the almost cool breeze.

Hully said, "Terry wouldn't've had to be an eyewitness to be dangerous to the killer. Everybody knew he
and Pearl were best friends. She might have confided
in Terry about something that allowed him to know, or
anyway strongly suspect, the murderer's identity."

Jardine nodded. "There's another possibility."

"Which is?"

They were passing by a shooting gallery where soldiers were throwing baseballs at milk cans, and sailors were playing Skee-Ball and pinball.

"Perhaps," Jardine said, "Terry Mizuha wasn't strictly *mahu*—maybe he was even closer to Pearl than we've been led to believe."

"Oh, that's crazy. . . ."

"Is it? Gates have been known to swing both ways, on this island. Suppose this jealous sailor pal of yours, or that soldier, came upon Terry and Pearl, together on the beach?"

"What, and confronted by a sudden act of violence, Terry fled?"

"Yes . . . and was afraid to come forward, for fear of looking a coward—hoping his silence would buy him a free pass from the killer."

"I don't buy it, John."

The detective summoned a thin smile. "Well, it's your own damn fault, Hully."

"My fault?"

"You're the one that started me thinking—I was content with Harry Kamana as the murderer."

Looking for Bill and Stanton, Hully and Jardine tried various taverns—the Two Jacks, the Mint, the New Emma Café—wading through clouds of cigarette smoke laced with the smell of stale beer, sorting swarms of sailors and soldiers, who were crowded at tables, packed in booths, flirting with Oriental waitresses, whom they so greatly outnumbered. None of the fresh, young, happy, sad faces belonged to Bill Fielder or Jack Stanton.

Hully and the detective checked tattoo parlors, where

boys sat bare-chested under bare bulbs as Filipino artists inscribed American flesh with hula girls, anchors
and "Mother." They tried curio shops where this sailor
bought a fringed pillow cursively designated "Honolulu," and that soldier purchased a monkey-pod carv-
ing. They tried storefront photo studios, where gobs
and GIs posed with pretty, grass-skirted Hawaiian girls
who had no interest in a date. They tried cafés—the
Bunny Ranch, Lousy Lui's, Swanky Franky—where
servicemen who had gotten drunk too fast tried to sober
up just as quickly.

No Fielder; no Stanton.

They tried a dime-a-dance joint, a barnlike second-
floor ballroom not unlike a church hall or an Elks club.
A small combo—piano, guitar, drums—played slow
tunes; tables were scattered on either side of the heavily
varnished, underlit cavern. Many of the girls were surprisingly good-looking, Hully thought, a variety of Japanese, Chinese, Puerto Rican, Hawaiian and
combinations thereof—also the occasional white girl—
in low-cut, shoulder-baring evening gowns. No liquor
was sold on the premises, nor was it allowed to be
brought in.

"These girls don't look like prostitutes," Hully whispered to Jardine, as the two stood on the sidelines.

"They aren't," the detective said. "See that blonde
over there?"

Jardine was indicating a dazzling blonde dancing
with an older man, a Filipino.

"She's somebody's wife, I'll lay odds," the detective
said. "These are nice girls. They aren't allowed to date

the customers—aren't allowed to leave until closing, when their mothers or their husbands pick them up."

But Hully wasn't looking at the blonde, anymore. He was nodding toward a soldier. "Hey—that's him. . . . That's Stanton."

Corporal Jack Stanton was dancing with an attractive if overly made-up Japanese girl in a low-cut blue satin gown that would have made her the hit of any prom; she was holding the boyishly handsome, brown-haired soldier close, her small fist tightly clenching a curling strand of tickets. She looked just a little bit like Pearl Harada, particularly to somebody drunk, like Jack Stanton.

When the tune ended—"Moonlight Becomes You"—Jardine went out onto the dance floor and tapped Stanton's shoulder, as if he were cutting in.

Stanton glared at the little fedora-sporting detective, but when Jardine held up his wallet, displaying his badge, Stanton swallowed and nodded, with morose inevitability. Hully couldn't hear what either man was saying—he had secured a small table at Jardine's request—and watched as the broad-shouldered, athletic-looking Stanton walked subserviently along with the diminutive detective, over to the waiting table.

Hully pulled out a chair for the corporal.

Suddenly Stanton's submissive attitude shifted; he seemed to bristle at the sight of Hully, saying, "I know you."

"I know you, too, Jack." Hully gestured to the chair and, in a not unfriendly way, said, "Sit down."

Stanton was scowling. "You're Bill Fielder's friend."

"I'm one of them."

Jardine said to Stanton, "Sit down." Not so friendly.

Stanton sat. He was inebriated, but short of sloshed. Jardine sat on one side of the soldier, Hully on the other.

The detective said, "I brought Mr. Burroughs along to identify you. I could have embarrassed you by going to your commanding officer and requesting a photo, you know."

Stanton's eyes narrowed. "Why didn't you?"

"I wanted to hear your story."

"What story?"

"The story of you and Pearl Harada."

Stanton swallowed. Then he put his elbows on the table and began to cry into his hands. The shabby little combo was playing "Fools Rush In."

Jardine gave the corporal a handkerchief. Stanton thanked Jardine and used it, drying his eyes, blowing his nose.

Then the detective said, "You and Bill Fielder got into a tussle over Pearl Harada last night. Want to tell me about it?"

Swallowing again, Stanton shrugged, saying, "It wasn't much of a 'tussle'—I punched him and he punched me. Then it got broke up. That's all."

"Why did you punch him?"

"Because . . . Pearl was my girl. I wanted him to stay away from her."

"You mean you were still seeing her? She was dating you, at the same time as Fielder?"

He shook his head, glumly. "No . . . no. She broke it

off with me, weeks ago. I just . . . couldn't get her out of my mind. Couldn't accept it. She was . . . so beautiful. So much fun . . . sweet . . . talented . . . smart . . ."

Jardine waited until Stanton stopped crying again, then said, "You were seen arguing with her last night."

"I know." Stanton worked up a sneer. "By that fairy Mizuha. He told you, right?"

Jardine's face was as impassive as a cigarstore Indian's. "The way this works is, I ask the questions. You argued with her?"

"It . . . it wasn't really an argument. I was . . . a little drunk. I yelled at her." The soldier leaned against an elbow, hand to his forehead, as if taking his own temperature. "She just looked at me, like . . . like she felt sorry for me. And maybe a little . . . disgusted . . . after I wouldn't stop yelling. I almost think that's what hurts most of all."

"What?"

"That she died thinking I was a jerk."

More tears followed, then Jardine asked, "Where were you, around twelve-thirty, one o'clock?"

"Back at Hickam."

"What time did you argue with Pearl?"

"Midnight—right after the band got finished."

"Where did you go, after the argument?"

"I told you—Hickam. I took a cab. I was in my rack by twelve-thirty, or damn close."

"You were in the barracks?"

"Yeah."

Jardine was jotting this down in his little notebook. Hully realized these assertions would be easily checked: the cab could be tracked; and whether or not Stanton had been in the barracks at the time of the girl's death. Pearl had been alive at twelve-fifteen, when she'd taken her leave of Hully's father, at their bungalow. And Hickam Field was twenty minutes from Waikiki.

If he was telling the truth, Stanton couldn't have been Pearl Harada's murderer.

"I want you at Central Police Station at ten o'clock Monday morning," Jardine said to the corporal. "For a formal statement. If you need to have your commanding officer call me, I work out of the Prosecutor's Office at City Hall."

And Jardine handed Stanton a business card. Stanton held it between thumb and middle finger and stared at it like a chimp trying to figure out a math problem.

Stanton's expression was one of astonishment. "You don't really think I . . . listen, I didn't . . . Do I need an attorney?"

"That's up to you, Corporal. If you were a prime suspect in my mind, I'd be taking you in right now."

He was shaking his head, his eyes as intense as they were red. "I wouldn't have hurt her. I would never have hurt her. I'd sooner kill myself. Do you have any idea what I'm going through? What it feels like inside my head right now? Inside my gut? My heart?"

"Monday. Ten o'clock."

"I thought Harry Kamana did it. Didn't you arrest him?"

"Ten o'clock. Monday."

Jardine rose and Hully followed suit.

"What about Fielder?" Stanton asked, still seated. "Where was he when Pearl was . . . ?"

"We're going to find that out," Jardine said. He touched the brim of his fedora, in a tip-of-the-hat manner, and headed for the door, Hully trailing after.

Just as they were going out, Hully saw Stanton heading back out to the dance floor with the Japanese girl, the combo playing, "I Got It Bad and That Ain't Good."

The Black Cat was a long, open-faced café that benefited from its proximity to the YMCA across the street, where buses and cabs had brought—and would later pick up—sailors and soldiers . . . anyway, those who weren't sleeping it off in a room in the big, rambling, palm-surrounded Y.

Sam Fujimoto was at a table right on the street with two sailors—one of whom was Bill Fielder. The other was Dan Pressman. The Black Cat served liquor, but all three were drinking coffee.

"Nice work," Jardine said to Sam, pulling up a chair, Hully doing the same.

Bill sat slumped in his chair, his expression dour, his handsome features puffy, his dark hair uncombed. Blond, blue-eyed Dan Pressman seemed more alert, and was watching Bill the way a parent watches a child. Hully's hunch was that Bill had been tying one on, and Dan had laid off the booze, to keep an eye on his friend's safety and welfare.

"Found Bill and Dan down at the Tradewinds," Sam said.

"Rough joint," Jardine said, and showed his badge

to the two sailors. "I'm Detective Jardine. How are you doing, Bill?"

"My fiancée was murdered," he said, just slightly slurring his words. "How the hell you think I am?"

"When did you see Pearl Harada last, Ensign?"

Dan said, "Detective, if you want to question Bill, don't you think it'd be more appropriate if you waited till he's—"

"I'll talk to him now," Bill said sharply. "Right now. I'm sober—sober enough. And I don't have a goddamn thing to hide."

"You should have a lawyer," Dan said. "This is a murder case."

Bill batted the air. "They already caught the guy. Didn't you catch the guy?"

"Harry Kamana is in custody," Jardine said. "When did you see Pearl last, Ensign?"

"At the Niumalu. I left about a quarter to midnight. . . . The Harbor Lights were still playing."

Jardine gazed out from under the shadow of the fedora brim. "She was your girl, wasn't she? Why didn't you hang around to spend some time with her, after?"

"I wanted to talk to my father. I was spending the weekend with my folks—and I knew I'd have the chance to talk to Dad about . . . about Pearl and me. About us getting married."

"Did you talk to him?"

"Yes." He shook his head, rolled his eyes. "Oh yes indeed."

"It did not go well?"

He grunted a humorless laugh. "It did not go well."

"What happened?"

Bill leaned forward, weaving slightly; his words remained slurred but coherent. "Just a shouting match. My mother tried to calm both of us down, but . . . I went to the guest room, slammed the door. That was the end of it."

"What time was this?"

"I got home just after midnight. We must have argued till one o'clock, one-fifteen."

Jardine glanced at Hully: this would seem to be an alibi for both Bill and his father . . . unless one was covering for the other.

"Ensign Fielder," the detective said, "I mean no disrespect . . . but you were not the only man in Pearl's life."

Bill slapped the metal table and the coffee cups jumped, spilling a little. "You're wrong! I *was* the only man in her life."

Jardine's voice was a persistent near monotone. "What about Jack Stanton? Harry Kamana?"

Bill gestured with an awkward hand. "They were old boyfriends. I didn't say she was a . . . a nun. But we were engaged—she wasn't dating anybody else, wasn't seeing anybody else. Just me."

"How would you have felt if you found her in the arms of another man?"

The ensign bobbed forward. "Would it make me want to kill somebody? Is that what you want to know? Sure, Detective . . ."

Touching his friend's arm, Dan said, "Bill—easy, now . . . watch what you're saying. . . ."

"I'd have wanted to kill the son of a bitch who was with her . . . not Pearl. Never Pearl. But that didn't happen, Detective, and it wouldn't happen, couldn't happen. She loved me, I loved her. We were engaged. She was going to be . . . my wife."

"What if you found her in the arms of Terry Mizuha?"

Bill blinked. "Why would she be in that queer's arms? What the hell kind of stupid question is that?"

Jardine handed Bill a business card. "That's my office number at City Hall. But I want you down at Central Police Station at eleven o'clock Monday morning. Can you remember that?"

"Yeah." Bill was looking at the business card, trying to make his eyes focus. "Why do you wanna talk to me again?"

"I want your formal statement. I don't think you did this thing, Ensign Fielder, but you are a suspect. You may wish to bring an attorney along."

Bill's head was rocking, slightly. "I don't understand this—Harry Kamana did it! He had goddamn blood all over himself! Somebody saw him do it, right? Why . . ."

"We can discuss this Monday. Show up sober, Ensign."

Then Bill was on his feet, raving, ranting. "You let that bastard Kamana out, I'll kill his ass! You understand? You wanna arrest me for a murder, you'll get your chance. . . ."

Dan also got to his feet, latching onto Bill's arm. "Take it easy, Bill. Just stop talking, goddamnit."

A male voice chimed in: "Did you kill her, Fielder? Did you murder my girl?"

As if he'd materialized, Corporal Jack Stanton was standing next to the table. Now Hully and Jardine were getting to their feet, as Stanton grabbed the startled Bill Fielder by his khaki blouse, with both hands.

"Why did you do it, Fielder?" Stanton demanded, his eyes crazed. "Was she throwing you over? Coming back to me?"

Bill threw the first punch. Then the two heartsick, drunken servicemen were slugging away at each other, flailing, stumbling out into the street, mostly missing, occasionally connecting. Within seconds a crowd of sailors and soldiers had formed around them, cheering them on.

Jardine was shaking his head, giving Hully a look. "Oh hell," he said wearily.

It was only a matter of minutes before the crowd turned itself into a brawling mob, sailors belting soldiers, soldiers smacking sailors. Fielder and Stanton were no longer visible, swallowed in the sea of white and khaki, with shouted obscenities mingling with cries of pain.

The gunshot froze them all.

Then their eyes turned to the little Portuguese detective who had fired his .38 revolver into the air. The sailors and soldiers did not have time to process this before the MPs and Shore Patrol descended, blowing whistles, shouting admonitions, arresting a few of them, the bulk scattering.

Hully found Bill Fielder in a pile on the pavement,

barely conscious, fairly battered; Stanton was nowhere to be seen. Hully and Dan Pressman—who had not gotten involved in the fracas—walked Bill to the table and sat him down.

Dan said to Hully, "Listen, I need to catch a liberty ship. You want me to haul him back to the *Arizona*?"

"No—I'll baby-sit him tonight," Hully said. "Clean him up, and let him sleep it off."

Jardine was talking to the Shore Patrol and the MPs, showing them his badge.

"You guys always have this much fun on Hotel Street?" Hully asked Pressman.

Dan grinned. "Every time."

# TWELVE

## *Party Crashers*

In the golden Hawaiian moonlight, Schofield Barracks—the largest military base in the United States—looked like a perfectly idealized American town, right off the cover of *The Saturday Evening Post* or the back lot of MGM. If it were not for the surrounding fields of sugarcane and pineapple, no one would guess the Hawaiian location; if it were not for the sentry-guarded entry, no one would take this for an Army post. Street after street was lined with stucco and brick houses on well-manicured lawns, ranging from bungalows to near mansions, depending on the ranks of their occupants, of course; and—set off in splendid isolation, like castles of the realm—massive brick structures for various military purposes.

Burroughs pulled up outside the gate, waiting for FBI agent Adam Sterling. He had called the agent at the Niumalu, where Sterling had been brooding in his bungalow, after an unsuccessful meeting with General Short on the *lanai* of the latter's home, at Fort Shafter, the Army administrative quarters just outside Honolulu.

"Well, get out here to Schofield," Burroughs had told the FBI man, from a phone booth outside a gas station with a magnificent view of Pearl Harbor that rivaled the Shuncho-ro's. "I have new information for the general, and I won't be able to get past the guard without your help."

Burroughs filled Sterling in on what he'd learned from Kuhn and Morimura, and the FBI man, excited, said he was on his way and hung up.

The writer had paused to look at the view, before driving to nearby Schofield. Pearl Harbor was spread out before him, warships moored in pools of yellow luminance, signal lights blinking back and forth, search beams stroking the sky.

A chatty little Japanese man in coveralls—who had introduced himself as Mr. Sumida, the service station's owner, and who had smiled during every moment of gas pumping and windshield cleaning—was also admiring the glittering view, as Burroughs paid for his gas.

"So beautiful," Mr. Sumida said. "Like great big Christmas tree!"

Somehow this observation was less than comforting, and now—as Burroughs waited for Sterling outside the Schofield gate—he wondered how his son and Sam Fujimoto were faring. About now they would be combing Hotel Street for Bill Fielder and Jack Stanton, and the writer was well aware of the potential perils of that sleazy strip of sin.

Sterling pulled up in a black Ford, government issue no doubt, and Burroughs left the Pierce Arrow and hopped in front, on the passenger side. The FBI man showed his ID to the guard and they soon were rolling through the lush, suburban "barracks."

"We're probably on a fool's errand, Ed," the FBI agent said. The rangy, square-jawed Sterling—who still reminded Burroughs of a hero from one of his own books—seemed frazzled at the end of this long day, his white linen suit rumpled, his tie a limp, wrinkled rag.

Sterling proceeded to tell Burroughs that when he'd arrived at Fort Shafter at seven, for a promised ten-minute audience with the general, both Mrs. Short and Mrs. Fielder were already seated in the general's car with its motor running, in the driveway, waiting to go to the party at the Schofield Officers' Club.

Short had been unimpressed with the transcript of the Mori radiophone call. "If this is code," the general had asked skeptically, "why do they talk in the clear about things like planes and searchlights?"

While the wives fretted and fumed in the car, Sterling had tried to make his case to Short and Fielder (who lived next door to the general).

"General Short thought the Mori call was 'quite an ordinary message,' " Sterling said to Burroughs, pulling into the officers'-club parking lot. "Nothing much to get excited about."

"And of course Fielder parroted that view," Burroughs said dryly.

"The worst of it is, the general said he appreciated my 'zeal,' but perhaps I was being 'too intelligence-conscious.' "

Burroughs, shaking his head, said, "Is there such a thing, with war hanging over us?"

"When it comes to matters like these," Sterling said, as he parked his car in the nearly filled lot, "it's easy to be wrong. . . . Morimura being a case in point, on my part."

Burroughs was getting out of the car. "You might have done better with General Short during working hours. When a man's wife is waiting for him in a car, dressed to the nines ready to go to a party, his judgment is easily impaired."

As they walked up to the entry of the unpretentious brick building, the FBI agent warned Burroughs: "The general was pretty patient with me at his house, all considering, but this interruption may be something else again."

Sterling had already explained that this was not just the club's weekly Saturday-night dance, but an annual cabaret-style benefit show put on by "talented young ladies" who worked on the post. Right now they could hear a small combo—piano, drums, guitar and bass fiddle—accompanying a thin female voice doing Ella Fitzgerald's "A Tisket a Tasket," passably.

Once inside, they peeked in at the wood-paneled dining room, which was decked out with ferns and floral arrangements, and every linen-covered table had fresh-cut flowers; between two lava-rock columns was the stage area, where various amateurs were coming up to sing and dance and do their best. The men in the audience were in dress uniform and the women in their fanciest gowns, and the club was brimming with brass—in addition to Short and Fielder, who were positioned up front (unfortunately), Burroughs spotted Major Durward Wilson of the 24th Infantry Division, Lieutenant Colonel Emil Leard, and Lieutenant Colonel Walter Phillips, Short's chief of staff.

"Wait in the bar," Sterling told Burroughs, who did as he was told, as the FBI man waded gingerly into the sea of high-ranking officers.

With the benefit show in full sway, the bar was empty, but for the bartender himself, and Burroughs ordered a root beer at the counter, and retreated to a booth.

A few minutes later, Sterling returned with both General Short and Colonel Fielder, neither of whom seemed happy. Nor did they did seem inclined to join Burroughs in the booth, and the writer crawled out and stood and apologized for interrupting their evening out.

"I hope there's a good reason for this, Mr. Burroughs," the slim, wiry general said tightly.

Burroughs jumped right in. "You already know about the Mori radiophone call, and the Jap Consulate burning its papers. What you don't know is that Otto Kuhn, the German 'sleeper' agent, is working with Vice Consul Morimura, in an effort to pin the murder of Pearl Harada on an innocent man."

The general frowned, but with interest. This news

perked Fielder's curiosity, as well. Short gestured to
the booth, said, "Let's sit down—I'd like to hear this."

Burroughs and Sterling sat across from the general
and the colonel. Both men seemed keenly attentive as
the writer told them what Kuhn had admitted about the
phone call, and that Morimura had flaunted his spying
activities, right down to the powerful telescope in his
private room at the Shuncho-ro.

Sterling said, "My office has clearly underestimated
Morimura—he's put on a good front as a womanizer
and buffoon. But it's apparent he's involved heavily in
spying, though much of it may be legal."

"This is intriguing information, Mr. Burroughs," the
general said, nodding thoughtfully. "But I as yet fail to
see a reason for your sense of urgency. . . ."

"Pearl Harada's uncle is on the FBI's list of dangerous Japanese-Americans here in Oahu. She may have
been involved in something having to do with espionage, or overheard something." Burroughs turned to
Fielder. "Wooch, that girl made a concerted effort to
have me arrange a meeting between the two of you."

Fielder shrugged. "Of course—because she and my
son wanted to get married. . . ."

This was news to Short, who looked sharply at
Fielder, who went on, faintly chagrined.

"My son and that girl knew I would forbid such a
union, and she wanted to try to win me over."

"That's right," Burroughs said. "And we've been assuming that she was going to bat her eyes and sweet-
talk you and just generally appeal to your basic
goodness . . . but Wooch, what if she was going to

prove herself to you by handing you sensitive information?"

Fielder's eyes narrowed, and so did Short's.

"I spoke to that girl minutes before her murder," Burroughs said. "She was anxious to see you, Wooch, as soon as possible. *She* had a real sense of urgency about her, let me tell you . . . and somebody else had enough of a sense of urgency to murder her before she could talk to you."

Fielder seemed stunned, trying to absorb this.

"What do you think she knew?" the general asked.

"I can only guess," Burroughs said. "But if the Japs, through Morimura, are waking their sleeper agent . . . literally . . . and murder is being committed, right down to framing some poor fall guy . . . it must be something important. Something . . . urgent."

"It would certainly seem that Morimura and Kuhn are worth serious investigation." General Short turned to Fielder, who was after all his top intelligence man. "First thing Monday morning, I want you to meet with Agent Sterling and whoever's handling this murder case."

"That would be Detective John Jardine of the Prosecutor's Office," Burroughs told the general, "but do you really think you should wait until Monday?"

Short raised an eyebrow. "Morimura is a diplomat— with protected status. If he's been involved in illegal espionage, that status dissolves. Kuhn we can simply have arrested. Nevertheless, we need to tread slowly, carefully."

Burroughs leaned forward in the booth. "General

Short, what if Pearl Harada had information indicating invasion was at hand?"

"Mr. Burroughs, war *is* at hand, unless these negotiations with the Japs start going someplace, quick . . . Washington indicates we could have hostile action at any moment."

"Well, then—"

"And I'm grateful to you, Mr. Burroughs, for this information indicating that espionage efforts here in Oahu are heating up."

The writer was shaking his head. "General, I'm not talking about war, I'm talking about *invasion*—a sneak attack. Your man Colonel Teske believed it would come by air at dawn on a Saturday or Sunday—when the Japs know they would have their best shot at finding our ships in port and many men off duty, our guard dropped."

"Our 'guard' is never dropped, Mr. Burroughs," the general said, crisply, defensive irritation unmistakable in his tone. "War is coming but almost certainly not in Hawaii—I asked my chief of staff just yesterday what the odds were of that, and he told me, flatly, 'Zero.' "

Then Short was out of the booth, Fielder too, the general thanking the writer for his patriotism and his conscientiousness.

"This activity by Morimura and Kuhn is unquestionably pertinent," he told Burroughs and Sterling, who were still seated in the booth. "We're on alert against sabotage, espionage activities and subversion right now. When the Japs attack—whether it's the Philippines or Borneo—we'll have to be ready to handle a bloody uprising of their local fifth column."

And, after a few polite smiles and nods, General Walter Short and Colonel Kendall Fielder were off to rejoin their wives, who were listening to a trio of girls from the camp PX singing "Boogie Woogie Bugle Boy."

"Hell, Ed," Sterling said, ashen, as the two walked out into the officers'-club parking lot in the still, crisp air, "if your hunch about invasion is correct, the general's antisabotage efforts could backfire tragically."

"How so?"

"Well, in this antisabotage alert he's implemented, Short's ordered ammo boxed up and locked, to prevent theft. And all the warplanes are disarmed and massed close together, in the middle of open tarmacs."

The writer's eyes popped. "Are you serious? That makes a perfect target for an enemy air raid!"

The FBI agent shrugged, glumly. "It's easier to guard the planes that way, Short says—against the 'fifth column' of local Jap saboteurs."

Burroughs shook his head. "And what I told him about Morimura probably only reinforced that notion."

As they headed out of Schofield in the black Ford, Burroughs said to Sterling, "We have to talk to Admiral Kimmel. We have to try him."

"That's probably not advisable. . . ."

"Do you know where he is tonight?"

"I do," Sterling admitted. "A party at the Halekulani, given by Admiral Leary and his wife."

A number of the Navy's top brass lived at the Halekulani Hotel.

"Drop me at my car," Burroughs said, "and I'll meet you over there—in the lobby."

Just beyond Fort DeRussey, on the ocean side of Kalia Street, the Halekulani was a low-key, casually posh hotel whose buildings and cottages seemed interwoven with the Hawaiian landscape. The House Without a Key bar was named after Earl Derr Biggers's first Charlie Chan mystery, a small resonance Burroughs might have savored, under less tense circumstances: John Jardine's late colleague on the Honolulu PD, Chang Apana, had been the basis for the fictional Chan.

Burroughs and the FBI agent found Admiral Kimmel in the company of Rear Admiral Draemel and Admiral Pye and their wives, sipping cocktails at a table under the big *hau* tree on the Halekulani terrace. A grouping of tables nearby made up a dinner party of around a dozen—all top brass and their wives . . . except, of course, for Husband Kimmel, whose wife was back on the mainland.

Sterling approached the stern, broad-browed admiral, apologizing for the intrusion, and politely asking for a few minutes of his time.

In the charming, pale pink, wicker-furnished lobby, standing near a huge window looking out on a seemingly impenetrable thickness of tropical garden, Burroughs and the FBI man laid out their cards for Admiral Kimmel. It took a while longer than the meeting with Short and Fielder, because Kimmel knew nothing of the Mori radiophone call, though he was aware of the Japanese Consulate burning their papers.

"That's only natural," the stately admiral said, a faint

touch of Kentucky in his voice, "at a time like this."

"With war imminent, you mean?" Burroughs said.

"Yes. Now what is this business about murder, and espionage?"

They filled him in slowly, and the admiral listened, absorbed, frequently nodding. Burroughs and Sterling exchanged occasional glances, both men feeling they were getting through to Kimmel.

But in the end, the admiral's reaction mirrored the general's.

"This begs prompt action," Kimmel said. "First thing Monday morning."

"Admiral Kimmel," Burroughs said, "Sunday is the perfect time for an invasion. . . ."

The admiral's clear blue eyes seemed tranquil. "The Japs may indeed invade, tomorrow—somewhere in Southeast Asia, that is."

"What about here? In Hawaii?"

"No one gives that possibility much credence. Just last week I asked my operations officer what the chances were, of a surprise attack on Oahu, and he said, 'None.' I hope you won't mind if I rely on the advice of our leading military minds and not . . . forgive me . . . the creator of Tarzan?"

The admiral thanked both men for their diligence, and returned to the terrace and the single cocktail he was conservatively making last all evening.

Soon the writer and the FBI man were back at the Niumalu, in their respective bungalows; when he took his leave, Sterling seemed weary and defeated. Burroughs felt about the same, but was relieved and even energized to find Hully at home. They had company: Hully had hauled his inebriated and somewhat battered friend, Bill Fielder, to sleep it off, which he was doing, on a pallet on the floor.

Father and son sat on the couch and exchanged their tales of the evening's investigations, each surprising, occasionally delighting, the other with revelations and adventures.

But finally it was left to Hully to ask, "What does it all add up to, O. B.?"

His father shrugged. "Harry Kamana is innocent—and so, most likely, are Bill and Stanton and the other 'jealous lovers.' Pearl Harada was killed for a classic motive: she knew too much."

"But *what* did she know, Dad?"

"I can't tell you, Son—and neither can Pearl."

Hully sighed. "I guess our investigation is over."

"Ours is—but when Sterling and Jardine get together with Colonel Fielder of Army intelligence, Morimura and Kuhn won't stand a chance."

"And when does this happen?"

"Monday."

"Monday." Hully stretched, yawned. "I guess it can wait that long."

And—with Bill snoring on his pallet on the floor—Hully folded out the couch into a bed, while his father trundled off in hopes of a good night's sleep, minus any nightmares or other rude awakenings.

# THREE:

*December 7, 1941*

# THIRTEEN

## *War Games*

After the midnight closing of the Navy's new Bloch Recreation Center—where the *Arizona*'s dance band had come in second to the *Pennsylvania,* a much-contested decision—and with the dimming of the clubs and bars of the city, garish Hotel Street included, the blush in the sky over Honolulu began to fade, until the heavens again belonged to the stars. Oahu itself seemed to slumber, with only the slowly turning hands of the Aloha Tower's quartet of clock faces to mark the passing of another tropical night.

By three A.M., the darkness was broken chiefly by stoplights pulsing red, and mute, deserted streets twinkling with Christmas lights. A few pleasure palaces in Chinatown ignored the curfew, their entryways scarlet with the neon promise of sin, beckoning foolish tourists and fearless servicemen. And offshore, to the west, at the entrance to Pearl Harbor, red and green buoy lights winked in the dark, as if they and the night shared a secret.

In these deceptively peaceful hours before dawn, out in the blackness beyond the reef, destiny was bearing down upon Oahu. Three hundred miles north of Honolulu, an armada charged through heavy seas at a clip of twenty knots—destroyers and cruisers, battleships and aircraft carriers, bombers and torpedo planes— while, much closer to Oahu, a small fleet of submarines already had the island surrounded, and five midget submarines were even now gliding toward their targets.

A little before four A.M., a minesweeper signaled the destroyer *Ward* of the sighting of a possible periscope three-quarters southwest of the harbor's blinking entrance buoys. General quarters were sounded by Lieutenant William Outerbridge, captain of the *Ward*— summoned to the bridge in his pajamas, over which he wore a kimono—and for half an hour, the destroyer searched the restricted waters outside the harbor, and saw nothing, their sonarmen hearing nothing.

Then at 6:30 A.M., a *Ward* crewman spotted the half-submerged midget sub trailing the supply ship *Antares* toward the harbor entry, whose torpedo nets—usually blocking the channel—were wide open. Lieutenant Outerbridge sounded general quarters again, and took chase, quickly closing to within a hundred yards, firing and missing, then—with a point-blank hit—nailing the sub at the juncture of its conning tower, sinking the seaweed-shrouded sub, then pounding it with depth charges until the wounded ship bled oil.

The *Ward,* little realizing it, had just fired the first shots of the Pacific War.

Though this encounter had taken place within five miles of Battleship Row, Oahu continued to slumber—Lieutenant Outerbridge, who of course promptly radioed a coded message of the sinking to the commander of the Fourteenth Naval District at Pearl Harbor—did not receive a request for "additional details" until 7:37 A.M.

Just before dawn, atop a ridge on the northern shore of Oahu, one of Colonel Teske's mobile radar stations was scheduled to be shut down at seven A.M. General Short had these half-dozen trailer-mounted units in operation only a few hours a day, primarily for training purposes. Private George Elliot and Private Joe Lockard were working a four-hour graveyard shift, three in the morning till seven; but the truck that was supposed to pick them up for breakfast was late, and Private Elliot left the equipment on after seven, merely for the practice.

And just as dawn was threatening to break, a notably strong wave pattern blipped on Elliot's five-inch-diameter oscilloscope, indicating dozens of aircraft, about 130 miles north, heading toward Oahu—at a speed, they soon estimated, of around 180 mph.

Elliot called this in to the Air Warning Service at Fort Shafter, where Lieutenant Kermit Tyler—assuming these blips represented some B-17s expected in from the mainland—told the radarman, "Well, don't worry about it."

Lockard suggested they shut down the radar set, but

Elliot wanted some more practice: he watched until the swarm of planes was only twenty-two miles north of Oahu, at which point the patterns disappeared. Unaware that this meant the planes were lost in the dead zone of the hills, as they crossed the shoreline, Elliot switched off the set and logged his final report, at 0740 . . .

. . . content that he'd had enough practice for one day.

The blips on his screen had been forty-three Zeros, forty torpedo bombers, and one hundred bombers, the first wave of planes launched at six A.M. by the Japanese battle fleet 275 miles due north of the radar station. Their shadows racing across the checkerboards of sugarcane and pineapple fields, the 183 silver planes streaked over the lushly tropical, dreamily peaceful island, where a harbor as still as a millpond awaited, part of a golden landscape basking in the tranquillity of a Sunday dawn.

At around 7:30 A.M., Hully Burroughs and his father sat at a round wicker table on the Niumalu patio, having breakfast. Hully was in his tennis whites, O. B. in a short-sleeved woven tan shirt and khaki slacks, an ensemble that looked vaguely military; both men were in sneakers. The plan was to play tennis after breakfast, so they again ate light—orange juice and coffee and muffins and fresh fruit.

Their houseguest, Bill Fielder, was still on the pallet in the bungalow, sleeping it off, dead to the world. The chief topic of discussion between father and son was their frustration that the Sunday paper was late: Hully's brother Jack's comic strip, based on ERB's John Carter of Mars stories, was making its debut today.

"Well, it's not like we haven't seen the proofs," Hully said, buttering a muffin.

"Sure, but I'm anxious to see it in color," O. B. said, obviously disappointed that he couldn't read this latest Burroughs spin-off—helmed by his eldest son, a fact of which he was inordinately proud—over his morning coffee.

Neither father nor son had mentioned anything about the murder investigation that had so consumed them the day before; this was a new day—witness the endless blue sky puffed with clouds, the surf rolling gently to shore, hear and feel the wind whispering through the fronds, a strangely still morning, quiet, serene . . . Sunday.

When the first sounds of artillery fire interrupted that serenity, shattering it even, Burroughs, coffee cup in hand, looked at Hully with one arched eyebrow.

"No," Hully said, to the unasked question.

And O. B. nodded.

After all, yesterday's papers had said that heavy guns would be fired from various parts of the island, over the next few days; and Oahu was a continual site of war games and realistic maneuvers.

As the sounds of battle built, other patrons of the Niumalu, at other tables, were exchanging the same information: *this was just a drill, some kind of Navy battle practice, or the Army having target practice. . . .*

A woman at a nearby table said in an English accent,

"What a wonderfully realistic imitation of a European air raid."

"Well, now I know how they sound," her male companion, an American, said matter-of-factly.

Soon, as father and son wandered to the tennis court, rackets in hand, Burroughs was saying, "You get used to these damn maneuvers, living on a military island like this. But I have to admit, after what we learned yesterday, I'm damned nervous. You don't think this could be . . ."

From the direction of the beach, the sky rumbled, and it wasn't thunder.

Nonetheless, Hully shook his head. "Dad, we'd be hearing sirens—it'd be all over the radio, by now. We'd know if this were more than just gunnery practice."

So they began to play tennis.

Before long, many of the Niumalu guests had gathered on the sandy patch adjacent to the tennis court, that sunbathing area where, not so long ago, Pearl Harada had lounged in a pretty pink bathing suit. From there, the rubberneckers could enjoy—just past the stubby wooden fence—a clear view of the coast, from Diamond Head to beyond Pearl Harbor and Barbers Point, though a hill kept them from seeing the Naval base.

Even from the court, Hully and his dad could quite plainly see—pausing between serves—bombs falling into the ocean not so far away, dense black smoke billowing up as if the water were on fire.

"It's a practice smoke screen," somebody said.

"Sure doesn't sound like practice," someone else said, rather idly.

Antiaircraft shells were exploding in the sky, and ships at sea were firing, and the guests were oohing and ahhing, as if at a Fourth of July fireworks display, marveling at these "realistic maneuvers the Navy was staging."

Hully had just returned a serve, and O. B. had swatted it back, when a bomb went off surprisingly nearby, and Hully's attention jerked toward the beach, the ball bouncing past him, unattended. The hotel guests were rearing back in horror and surprise. Gasps and screams intermingled as they began to back away, and gradually turned and walked, and ran, to their bungalows or the lodge or just somewhere else, anywhere else, as long as it was inland.

At the sound of that nearby explosion, Hully had tossed his racket and his father had done the same, and as the guests rushed toward them, the Burroughs duo moved through the panicking crowd, swimming against the tide, running toward the beach.

Fred Bivens, eyes wide and unbelieving, came up to them, gesturing numbly toward the waters.

"A supply ship—it was standing just offshore, by Fort DeRussey.... A bomb blew the damn thing up! What kind of war games are these?"

Hully and his father looked out and could see bombs bursting over Pearl Harbor and Hickam Field.

"It's war, Fred," O. B. said gravely. "Not games."

Hully grabbed his father by the arm and said to him pointedly, "Then let's go take a prisoner."

O. B., understanding, nodded curtly, and they took off.

Feeling like idiots—they if anyone should have known this was the real thing—Hully and O. B. ran toward the Kuhns' cottage. As they passed by an open window of another bungalow, a radio blasted out an announcer's call to action: *"All men report to your post! Calling all nurses! Proceed to Pearl Harbor!"*

And as they jogged by another open window, on another turned-up radio, a different announcer was saying, *"Civilians—stay off the street! Stay home! Do not use the telephone! Oahu is being attacked—the sign of the Rising Sun is to be seen on the wings of the attacking planes!"*

No radio was on in the Kuhns' quarters, but they found the door open and, inside, Adam Sterling, who had a .38 revolver in his right hand. The place was a mess, almost as if it had been searched; but that wasn't exactly the case.

The FBI agent, who might have been a tourist in his aloha shirt and chinos, looked at them and said, "Kuhn and his wife cleared out, sometime during the night."

Hands on his hips, O. B. snorted a laugh and asked, "Where the hell do they think they're gonna hide, on this island?"

Sterling stuck the gun in his waistband, shrugging. "Maybe with Jap sympathizers. Maybe they think that fifth column is going to rise up, or maybe an invasion is going to follow this goddamn air raid, and they're hiding till the outcome." Swallowing thickly, Sterling shook his head and his eyes locked with O. B.'s. "Jesus, Ed—did we *have* to be right?"

Explosions, muffled, underscored the agent's statement.

"This is it," O. B. said through clenched teeth. "This is the attack. But my question is—is *this* what Pearl Harada knew?"

Sterling shook his head. "No—but close. Last night, after you and I struck out with General Short and Admiral Kimmel . . . and what a morning I bet they're having . . . I couldn't sleep. So I went over to the dining room, where the Harbor Lights were dragging their behinds through a performance . . . two of their members murdered, what a damn pall that cast."

"I can imagine," Hully said.

"Yeah," O. B. said to the FBI agent, "but what the hell does that—"

Nodding, the FBI man picked up his train of thought. "I talked to a young man in the band who, as it turns out, was . . . secretly . . . Terry Mizuha's *other* best friend." He grunted a humorless laugh. "Hell, why mince words at a time like this? Terry Mizuha's boyfriend—his lover."

O. B.'s eyes narrowed to slits. "What did this 'lover' tell you?"

Distant explosions continued to accentuate the FBI agent's words.

"Terry had confided in him, Ed—just like Pearl had confided in Terry. Nonspies aren't much at keeping secrets, you know. Seems our esteemed Japanese vice consul, Tadashi Morimura, is not a diplomat at all—

he's a spy named Takeo Yoshikawa. A top espionage agent. . . So much for 'legal' spying."

O. B. and Hully exchanged glances; then O. B. asked, "Is that an act of war? Having a spy pose as a diplomat?"

Sterling barked a hollow laugh. "Kind of a moot point right now, don't you think?"

And an especially loud explosion seemed to agree.

The FBI agent gestured to a telephone on a small table. "Listen, the hotel phones are out. Maybe some Jap plane snagged the phone lines. So I can't call the office, and anyway it's just a skeleton crew over there; and I can't contact anybody at home, obviously. I'm on my own—you and Hully want to help?"

Hully was nodding, emphatically, as O. B. said, "Sure—how?"

Sterling's smile had a sneer in it. "I want to get over to that Japanese embassy and arrest that son of a bitch, Morimura/Yoshikawa, plus I want to take all those other Nips into custody, right down to General Counsul Kita. . . . You got a gun, Ed?"

O. B. nodded. "I still have Otto's Lüger—in the bungalow."

"Get it. That is, if you want to help out."

"Oh, I want to help." Eyes so tight they seemed to be shut, O. B. stood almost nose to nose with the FBI agent (or would have if Sterling hadn't been so much taller) and said, "Listen, Adam—Pearl knew more than just Morimura's last name, I'm sure of it. That bastard Morimura or Yoshi-something *knew* about this attack. This invasion got Pearl killed, and that Terry fella as well—they're the first casualties of this new war. Well, the Army and Navy have their hands full right now— you bet we'll be glad to help the FBI get that bastard."

Sterling and Hully tagged along as O. B. headed back to the bungalow to get the German's gun. As they approached, Bill Fielder—in his bare feet, his green sportshirt unbuttoned, zipping his chinos—came tumbling out, bumping into Hully.

The young ensign's face was unshaven, his eyes red, his dark hair sticking out here and there with sleep-induced cowlicks.

"Christ, have you heard?" Bill asked.

With bombs bursting in air—just like "The Star Spangled Banner"—this was a fairly absurd question.

"It's no drill," O. B. said.

"I gotta get to the *Arizona,*" Bill said desperately, wheeling from Hully to O. B. to Sterling. "You gotta drive me there! I gotta get in this! I gotta help!"

"Keys to the Pierce Arrow are on the coffee table," O. B. said, pointing to the nearby screen door. "Take it—try not to get my buggy shot the hell up . . . or yourself."

"Thank you, thank you," Bill murmured, and ran back inside the Burroughs cottage.

Sterling paused for just a moment, watching Bill through the screen, and Hully was surprised to see that the FBI agent—this strong-jawed six-foot-two Tarzan type—had tears welling.

"The men on those ships getting bombed," he said softly, voice catching, "they're all boys like that—average damn age is nineteen."

O. B. whispered, "Dying out there, right now."

Then Bill, clutching the car keys, came streaking past them, flashing a nod of thanks and a grimace of a smile.

Burroughs went in and retrieved the Lüger, and followed after as the FBI man dashed toward the crushed-coral parking lot where the Ford waited, Hully right there at his father's side.

"Didn't miss the fire this time, Dad," he said.

"Wish to hell I had," O. B. said.

There were tears in his father's eyes, as well; but—as was the case with the FBI man—Edgar Rice Burroughs's jaw was firmly set.

# FOURTEEN

## *Under Fire*

At the same time as Edgar Rice Burroughs and his son Hulbert were sitting down for breakfast at the Niumalu, two barefoot young fishermen were settling in on the enlisted men's landing at Pearl City. Sitting on the pier in only their khaki trousers, having yanked their T-shirts off (once they'd slipped out of their mother's sight), the Morton boys—Don, eleven, and Jerry, thirteen—did not brandish poles: instead, they unfurled a simple ball of string out into the water.

The boys were old hands at this, though they were resigned to slim pickings, even if on occasion they had managed to snag a hapless perch; and while the morning's fishing would certainly be on the dull side, Don and Jerry would no doubt be entertained by the harbor's always interesting parade of ships and sailors, planes and pilots. . . .

Puffs of wind gently stirred the glassy surface of the

water, and the sun peeked from behind cotton-candy clouds, promising a hot, lazy day—a typical Sunday for the two boys, although the fish did seem to be biting, for a change.

Seeking more bait, Don scrambled up to their house, only two hundred yards from the landing, while Jerry lounged in the golden sunlight, squinting as he took in a view any kid might relish, the ships of the Pacific Fleet strewn before him like so many toys in his tub. Groupings of destroyers convened about their tenders, to the north and east; and cruisers faced into the Navy Yard piers, at the southeast. Farther south lay the cruiser *Helena,* and—in dry dock with two destroyers— the battleship *Pennsylvania.* To the west were more destroyers, in and out of dry dock.

Lording over it all, in the middle of the harbor, sat Ford Island, where even now the boys' stepfather was on duty at the seaplane hangars. Patrol planes and carriers were stationed there, carriers moored on the northwest side, battleships on the southeast. Only today, Jerry noted, the carriers were all out at sea.

But there was still plenty for a kid to look at—the *Utah,* a battleship turned target ship; the seaplane tenders *Swan* and *Tangier;* the mine layer *Ogala;* cruisers like the *Raleigh, Helena* and *Detroit;* the old gunboat *Sacramento* with its thin, old-fashioned smokestack; and—on the far side of Ford Island—an exciting lineup of funnels and masts, the "trees" of Battleship Row, the *Arizona, California, Maryland, Nevada, Oklahoma, Tennessee,* and *West Virginia.* What other kid's bathtub armada could compare to that?

Still, all of this was old news to Jerry, who was glad the fish were biting. Otherwise, this had the makings of another really dull Sunday—that must have been why somebody was playing with firecrackers, off in the distance someplace.

Twenty miles east of where Jerry and Don were fishing, on the windward coast of the island, Japanese fighter planes and dive-bombers were swooping down on Kaneohe Naval Air Station.

One moment all was quiet, the next men were running after guns and ammunition, shouting, cursing, as the enemy planes made scrap metal out of the big PBY patrol planes at the station, moored to buoys in the bay and sitting unmanned on ramps.

Thirty-three Army planes were either damaged or destroyed.

All were in flames.

Don Morton was halfway down to the pier from the house, bringing more bait, when an explosion pitched him onto his face. The eleven-year-old covered his ears, his head, as three more blasts rocked the world over and around him.

Then, scared spitless, he scurried back up the slope and ran inside the house, just as his mother was coming out, her face white, her eyes wide.

Standing there in the doorway, she leaned down, putting her hands on his shoulders. "Go down and fetch your brother—now! Hurry!"

Don did as he was told, even as planes were gliding

by overhead, housetop level. The boy heard gunfire and realized it was coming from above, and the dirt road nearby puffed up, making little dust clouds, as the pilot strafed the area.

As dust danced on the road, Don—momentarily frozen—yelled, "Jerry!"

And then the boy turned and ran back to the house, and his mommy. When he got there, Don saw their next-door neighbor, a Navy lieutenant, in his p.j.'s., out on his own front yard.

The funny thing was, the grown man was crying too, crying for *his* mommy.

FBI agent Sterling was at the wheel of the black Ford with Burroughs in front, and Hully was in the backseat, sitting forward, like a kid.

As they headed for the Japanese Consulate, downtown, Burroughs was dismayed to see civilians failing to take cover, standing out in their yards and on the sidewalks, staring skyward, pointing at the plumes of black smoke, some laughing, convinced they were watching the military training exercise to end all such exercises.

Perhaps they were, he thought.

At first the traffic was nonexistent, the streets vacant, spookily, ominously so; and as the spectators began to get the point—as radios around the city informed them this was "the real McCoy!"—the citizens of Honolulu scrambled inside, leaving the sidewalks and front yards empty, as well.

For several blocks, the emptiness—punctuated by

the muffled sound of explosions—was eerie, almost as if the world had ended, leaving behind only brick and concrete.

Suddenly, vehicles were everywhere, speeding, careening, civilian autos and taxicabs packed with sailors and soldiers desperate to get back to their ships and posts, delivery vans and ambulances and fire trucks, sirens screaming. . . .

Soon the FBI agent's Ford was snarled in traffic.

Sterling, pounding the wheel impatiently, turned to Burroughs. "You really think Yoshikawa alias Morimura knew today was the day?"

Burroughs shrugged, sighed; the German's little automatic was in his hand. "Maybe not. Maybe he just knew that some Sunday soon, Oahu would be the target."

Sterling's smile was bitter; he shook his head. "All I keep thinking is 'poinsettias and hibiscus.' "

From the back, Hully said, "That radiophone call?"

"Code," Burroughs said.

Sterling nodded. "Code, all right—for certain kinds of ships."

Burroughs glanced at his son. "Maybe that bastard did know—our esteemed vice consul."

Traffic began to move again—as sirens wailed, and the sky roared.

"If we can ever get to the Consulate," Sterling said, through tight teeth, "we'll just ask the son of a bitch."

On a windy plain ten miles north of Pearl Harbor lay Wheeler Field, the Pacific's largest American fighter base. U-shaped barricades had been constructed to protect Wheeler's nearly one hundred fighter planes, Army Air Force P-40s and P-36s; this morning, however, the planes were clustered on the runways, wingtip to wingtip—playing out General Short's antisabotage strategy, a policy the other Oahu bases were following, as well.

Japanese planes pounced on the sitting ducks, dropping bombs, unleashing cannon fire and machine-gun blasts, chewing up the rows of parked fighters, fuel tanks igniting, leaving the hangars, enlisted men's barracks and PX in flames.

Dive-bombers swooped so low, inflicting their damage, that phone lines got snagged, and men on the ground could see the gold teeth in the grins of Jap pilots as they flashed by. No time to fight back, unarmed airmen died in their beds, or running for their planes, or for safety, though the base had no air-raid shelters. Their ammunition—locked away to keep local saboteurs from getting it, courtesy of General Short—was out of reach, stored in one of the burning hangars, bullets popping like popcorn in the conflagration.

Then the planes soared away, leaving thirty-nine men dead, and many more wounded.

Just north of Wheeler, at the suburban sprawl that was Schofield Barracks, sounds resembling explosions roused the interest of soldiers, who—upon glancing outside the mess hall—saw a plane with a black canopy and fuselage marked with a red spot, circling the roof of the building housing HQ.

Breakfast trays in hand, several soldiers were arguing over whether this was a Jap plane or some strange Navy craft, when buglers trumpeted an alert. The men tossed their trays and ran from the mess hall into the quadrangle; others sought out rifles, and two artillery-men ran to the rooftop and fired at planes with Browning Automatic Rifles, emptying clips at the dive-bombers.

One of the Jap planes crashed.

Cheers went up.

Then a new topic of conversation took over among the frightened young soldiers: how much would it hurt to be shot by a Jap bullet? Was it true the Nips only used .25 caliber ammo?

Admiral Kimmel had gotten up early on this fine Sunday morning; every other weekend, he would meet with General Short for eighteen holes of golf. Today, Lieutenant Colonel Throckmorton and Colonel Fielder would be joining them.

He'd recently moved into this house at Makalapa Heights, about five minutes from HQ, and the place was underfurnished—severely lacking the touch his wife would have brought to it. On days off like this, he missed her dearly; but most of his time was so filled with work, he scarcely remembered he had any private life.

This week had been filled with protracted discussions over whether the fleet should be kept in Pearl Harbor or sent to sea; and now this business was looming of the supposed espionage activities that Adam Sterling—a good man, if overeager—and the ever-imaginative Ed Burroughs had brought to his attention last night.

He was still in his pajamas, and hadn't even shaved yet, when Commander Murphy, duty officer at HQ, called to say the *Ward* had ash-canned a sub near the harbor.

"Sorry to bother you on Sunday morning, sir," Murphy said.

Kimmel realized this was probably just another false alarm—incorrect reports of subs in the outlying area were common.

But he said, "You acted correctly, Commander—all submerged sub contacts must be regarded as hostile. . . . I'll be right down."

Around five minutes later, freshly shaved and just getting into uniform, Kimmel again answered the phone and once more it was Murphy.

But this time the businesslike commander's voice was strangely shrill: "Sir, we have a message from the signal tower saying the Japanese are attacking Pearl Harbor—and this is no drill!"

Kimmel slammed the phone down and ran outside, onto the front lawn, into the garden which overlooked the base, buttoning his white uniform jacket as he went.

The sky was filled with the enemy—the Rising Sun on their wings. He knew at once this was no casual raid, by a few stray planes.

"Unbelievable," he murmured.

Aghast, he stood frozen among the flowers—poinsettias and hibiscus in bloom—watching Jap aircraft swoop down on the base, circling in figure eights, dropping bombs, turning and dropping more, machineguns chattering. Explosions rocked the sky—and ships, fires already burning fiercely on their decks.

"Impossible," he whispered.

Four miles west of Pearl Harbor, the Ewa Marine Corps Air Station was hit by two squadrons of silver planes bisecting the field at two hundred mph, fishtailing to better lash their bullets into broad patterns.

Of the base's forty-nine fighters and scout planes, thirty were decimated on the ground.

Four blocks from Beretania Street, the black Ford managed to crawl through the traffic jam and make it across Kuakini Street, bordering Pauoa Park, where on the left-hand corner squatted the two-story concrete compound of the Japanese Consulate.

Sterling pulled up in front, into the no-parking zone, and Burroughs and his son hopped out, following the FBI agent up the stairs, where—oddly—Consul General Nagao Kita stood halfway down . . . in his dark blue silk pajamas.

Burroughs had met the usually affable Kita before, socially, as had Sterling—the consul general was short, plump, with dark thick hair, and a broad, bushy-browed face that, with its flattened pug nose, gave him the appearance of a cheerful ex-prizefighter.

"Good morning, gentlemen," Kita said, arms folded, smiling like a friendly genie.

"Don't you know there's a war on?" Sterling demanded.

Kita shrugged. "This is just another American exercise—an elaborate one, I admit."

"Take a look at the color of that smoke," Sterling said, nodding toward the sky. "It's black, not white—fuel oil. Your planes are bombing Pearl Harbor."

"Nonsense."

"I'm going to have to take you in custody, Mr. Kita. We're at war, and I have evidence of espionage on the part of your vice consul."

The smile disappeared into an impassive mask. "I'm a diplomat, Mr. Sterling. Even if we are at war—I have certain rights."

"You have no rights—American boys are dying right now in this vicious underhanded attack. Where is your vice consul? Where is Yoshikawa?"

Kita's eyes tightened. "I know no one by that name."

"I'll settle for Morimura, then."

A siren screamed and tires squealed as a police car came to a halt next to the black Ford. Three uniformed police officers—two Hawaiians and a Chinese—jumped out, shotguns in hand, and so did a plainclothes officer . . . Detective John Jardine, a .45 automatic in his fist.

Jardine took the steps two at a time and joined the little discussion group, nodding to Burroughs and Hully, then saying to Sterling and Kita, "We're putting this building under armed guard."

"Why?" Kita said, his impassive face finally offering up a frown.

"For the protection of the consul general," the Portuguese detective said, "and the members of your staff."

Kita lifted a bushy eyebrow. "And if I don't want your protection?"

Jardine's wide thin mouth made a faint smile. "Well, we could wait an hour or so, for a nice mob to build, and then throw your ass to it."

That seemed to sober Kita, who said, "Shall we step inside?"

"What a good idea," Jardine said, then turned to the FBI man, who was already holding open the door. "Agent Sterling, we intend to fully cooperate with your office. If I might ask, why are Mr. Burroughs and his son with you?"

"I had to press them into service," Sterling said, as they allowed Kita to lead the way into the vestibule. "I've been cut off from my office."

"Glad to have your help," Jardine said, nodding at both Burroughs and Hully. "But why do I have the feeling we're still working the Pearl Harada murder case?"

"Help us find Vice Consul 'Morimura,' " Burroughs said, "and you'll find out."

A guard fence separated Pearl Harbor from the two thousand acres of Hickam Field, biggest Army base on Oahu, home of the Army's bomber squadrons. Here, a quarter mile of neatly arranged A-20s, B-17s and B-18s served themselves up to the hungry waves of silver planes.

The incessant bombing and strafing—not only of the

sitting-duck aircraft but barracks, support facilities and hangars—did not dissuade the men of Hickam from working fiercely to disperse their aircraft, or from fighting back.

Two Japanese-American civilians—laborers employed at the field—helped set up a machine gun and fed it with ammo belts while a boy from Michigan fired away at the diving planes.

Standing near a hangar, Corporal Jack Stanton—one eye slightly swollen, even blackened, from his Hotel Street brawl of the night before—saw the friend standing next to him strafed into explosive splashes of blood, bone and flesh. Horrified, then energized into action, Stanton ran across the tarmac—not even pausing when another bomb blew a khaki-clad soldier in two—and managed to climb up into a bomber.

Stanton began firing the machine gun in the nose of the bomber, its deadly chatter knocking one of the silver planes out of the sky.

But when a Zero swooped down, delivering its own machine-gun fire, the fuel tank ignited and Stanton was trapped in the cockpit, flames all around him, caged in a crackling hell.

Stanton didn't bother trying to get out. As the flames slowly consumed him, he kept firing up at the sons of bitches, and witnesses said his red tracer bullets could be seen zinging skyward, long after flames had encompassed the nose of the plane.

Winging eastward in groups of three, past the Pearl Harbor entry, cutting inland at an altitude of a mere

sixty feet, twenty-four torpedo planes threw their sup-
ple blue shadows across the Navy Yard and the Southeast Loch, closing in on Battleship Row—where those
gray behemoths, the *Arizona, California, Maryland,
Nevada, Oklahoma, Tennessee,* and *West Virginia,*
pride of the Navy, slumbered in the sunlight. In groups
of two, coming from the west, sixteen more torpedo
planes took a direct route across the island, their targets
the ships docked on the far side of Ford Island, as well
as those at the Navy Yard piers over the east channel.

Aboard the battleships, barely awake sailors per-
ceived the approaching attack planes as nothing more
than specks—but those specks grew ever larger as they
zeroed in on the harbor, crisscrossing. Swabbies—like
civilians—at first dismissed the planes . . . *crazy Army
pilots, damn Navy fliers showboating, ain't that a hell
of a drill. . . .*

"That's no star on the wing!" a sailor or two, on
every ship, would finally say, more or less. "That's a
red ball!"

And sailors, scattering like naughty kids caught in
some act, yelled, "It's the Japs! It's for real! It's war!"

PA systems barked orders, bugles blared, ships'
alarms trilled, and on every vessel in the harbor—130
of them—all hell broke loose, from the startled sailors
on deck who had seen the planes "dropping fish" (torpedoes) to the poor bastards sleeping in on Sunday who
had to tumble out of their racks, and scurry to their
battle stations, pulling on their clothes as they went.

Five torpedoes, in rapid succession, blasted the

*Oklahoma,* sending the battleship rolling slowly, inevitably to port. Breakfast dishes went flying, shattering, mess tables upended, lockers spilled open, and in the belowdeck barbettes, massive gun turrets tore free from their housings and tumbled grindingly down the slanting platforms, crushing crewmen.

When eleven-year-old Don Morton—frightened by the low-flying, strafing planes—came scooting back home without his brother Jerry, his mom wasn't mad. She just hustled him into their car and they drove down to the landing, where Don and Jerry had been fishing.

No other cars were around, but she honked her horn all the way, and Don thought maybe she was scared, too—they were driving right toward where all the explosions were coming from.

Suddenly Jerry came bursting out from some algarroba bushes, calling, "Mom! Mom!"

She stopped the car, let Jerry in, and hugged him.

"A man helped me," Jerry said. "He pushed me into the bushes when a plane was coming."

"What man?" his mother asked.

"That man," Jerry said, and pointed to the body of a Marine corporal alongside the dirt road.

Don's mom turned their car around and headed for Honolulu, as explosions shook the world all around them.

Bill Fielder, in the borrowed Pierce Arrow convertible, had a hell of a time trying to get to Pearl. He was crazy with desperation—all he could think of was getting back to his ship!

But it was a slow go. At first the streets were empty, but quickly they became clogged with cars and taxis, as well as emergency vehicles. Bill would whip his car around the jams, whenever possible, riding on the sidewalk if he had to. The sky boiled with black oil smoke, and it seemed like the end of the world—he passed by several water mains that had broken, shooting geysers fifty feet in the air, and people had loaded their cars up with toys and clothes, sometimes with baby buggies or bicycles strapped on the roof, like European war refugees, heading for the hills.

The rolling lanes of the Kamehameha Highway were choked with civilian cars and taxis piled with servicemen scrambling to get to their posts. It seemed to take forever, crawling toward Pearl Harbor. Finally, when he came over a rise, at the highway's highest point, he got a panoramic view: silver planes skimming over the sea toward battleships, bombs whistling down, dive-bombers howling in on their targets, shells exploding in midair, machine guns chattering, low-flying fighters strafing anything and everything, the harbor a mass of fuel oil, smoke and flames. Even from this distance, the acrid smell of burning and battle seemed to singe his nostrils.

The worst of it was the battleships getting hit so hard—the *Oklahoma* had already capsized, and the *Arizona* could be next.

He felt sick—at heart, to his stomach.

"Come on, come on, come on!" Bill yelled, and he

laid on his horn—not that honking would do any good. Everyone caught in this jam wanted it to move along just as badly as Bill did. But he was frustrated, knowing that time was running out.

He just wasn't aware how soon.

A bomb hit the Pierce Arrow, obliterating it, and Bill, leaving a charred, flaming husk of an automobile and very little of its driver.

Bill Fielder had just become the first *Arizona* fatality.

Moored aft of the *Tennessee,* a massive 608 feet long, the *Arizona* carried a main armament of twelve fourteen-inch guns, her hull shielded at the waterline by a thirteen-inch thickness of steel, with twenty inches of armor housing her four turrets. No more formidable weapon of war-at-sea was known to man than a battleship such as this.

An armor-piercing bomb hit the ship between its number-two gun turret and bow, punching a hundred-foot hole in the deck, then exploding in a fuel tank below. Within seconds, almost two million pounds of explosives detonated, forming a fireball of red, yellow and black, the ship lifting twenty feet in the air, tossing men like rag dolls, ship's steel opening like a blossoming flower to spread petals of huge red flame.

The halves of the ship tumbled into the water, where her skewed decks were walked by burning men, a ghostly, ghastly crew staggering out of the flames, one by one, dropping dead.

Seaman First Class Dan Pressman—whose previous battle had been on Hotel Street, last night—had been manning a gun-director unit above the bridge, when he sustained burns over most of his body; still, he managed to make use of a line that had been made fast to the mast of a repair ship moored alongside the *Arizona.*

Pressman and five other badly burned sailors—suffering shock, but wanting to live—swung high above the water on the line, going hand over hand to safety, even as their ears were filled with the screams of fellow crew members on the burning, dying halves of the ship, or in the water beneath, which, surrealistically, was on fire, too.

Her superstructure enfolded in flame, the *Arizona*—her shattered foremast tipping forward—settled to the bottom of the harbor, three-quarters of her crew. . . . some 1,177 officers and enlisted men . . . dead in the most devastating of all the blows delivered by Japan in the surprise air attack on Pearl Harbor.

In his quarters at Fort Shafter, General Short had just gotten into his golfing gear, for the planned eighteen holes with Kimmel, Fielder and Throckmorton, when he heard explosions—which he recognized at once as bombs going off.

He didn't think anything of it—the Navy was obviously having some sort of battle practice, and he was mildly annoyed that no one on Kimmel's team had warned him about it . . . unless they had told him, and he'd forgotten it.

But the explosions seemed to build, grow nearer, and that got the general's curiosity up. He wandered out onto his *lanai*—the very porch where the evening before an FBI agent had told him about a possible coded message—and he could see smoke to the west, a lot of it . . . and black.

Shrugging, he was heading back in to have some coffee before he left for the golf course, when he heard a loud knock at the front door. His wife was not up yet, so he went to answer it quickly, in case she had somehow managed to sleep through the Navy's infernal racket.

Wooch Fielder, in blue sport shirt and blue slacks, was standing on the front porch. Fielder had the startled expression of a deer perked by the sound of a hunter, and his face was fish-belly white.

"What's wrong, Wooch? Am I late?" The general looked at his wristwatch. "Didn't think we were playing till—"

"Sir, we're under attack—it's the real thing."

More explosions.

The general leaned out the door, asked, "What's going on out there?"

"Bicknell says he saw two battleships sunk."

"Why, that's ridiculous. . . ."

"Sir, both Hickam and Wheeler have phoned—they've been hit."

Short drew in a sharp breath; then, crisply, he said, "Put into effect Alert Number Three. Everybody to battle position."

"Yes, sir."

"Do it, Wooch—I'll be right with you."

And he shut the door, reeling, knowing that if the Japs would mount a damn-fool sneak air raid, they might even risk landing troops; there was no telling how seriously this attack might develop.

General Short knew only one thing for certain: he had to get out of these damn golf togs.

Don and Jerry Morton's mother, terrified by the explosions around them, stopped the car, and led her boys into a sugarcane field, where they all sat with hands on their ears, heads between their knees.

Now and then, Don's mother would ask either him or Jerry to peek up and see if the airplanes swooping overhead were American.

And, for the next two hours, they never were. Shivering, Don wondered if his stepfather was okay on Ford Island.

(He was not: the boys' stepfather had been among the first to die today, hit by a bomb on the Ford Island seaplane ramp.)

The U.S. Pacific Fleet was a family of sorts—big, and yet small enough that most men knew anyone else in their specialized line of work; a man might enlist and stay on one ship until retirement, twenty or thirty years later. Officers had ties, as well, often going back to Annapolis days. Admiral Kimmel knew thousands of his men by sight, and hundreds by name, and dozens were his personal friends.

From his office window at fleet HQ, Kimmel could do little more than stand and watch his ships . . . and his men . . . die—the admiral helplessly hearing the thunder of exploding bombs, and the anvil clangs of torpedoes ravaging his ships, bleeding rolling clouds of smoke.

His people tried to establish communications with the areas under attack, and sent messages to ships at sea, advising them of what was happening at Pearl. They could hear explosions and see waterspouts and, of course, the funnels of black smoke.

"I must say," Kimmel said quietly to the officers around him, "it's a beautifully executed military maneuver . . . leaving aside the unspeakable treachery of it."

As he stood there, a bullet came crashing through the window and struck him on the chest—leaving a sooty splotch on his otherwise immaculate white uniform. He bent to pick up what turned out to be a spent .50-caliber machine-gun slug.

Softly, he said, "I wish it had killed me—that would've been merciful."

Then he reached up and, with both hands, tore loose the four-star boards on his shoulders; he went into his office and came back wearing two-star boards, having demoted himself.

At the Japanese Consulate, Jardine and Sterling—with Burroughs and Hully tagging after—searched the compound. General Consul Kita was along, as well, a bored fat man in his pajamas; and when Jardine came to a locked door, toward the rear of the main building, he demanded that Kita open it.

"I have no key," Kita said, unflappable.

The acrid smell of smoke was leaching out from around the door.

"They're burning papers again," Sterling said. "Kita, tell them to open up!"

Sighing, seemingly blasé, Kita began to knock, but no one answered; Burroughs yanked the man aside, and Sterling crashed his shoulder into the wood, several times, until the door finally splintered open.

Four Japanese men in sport shirts and slacks were standing around a washtub in which they had been burning papers and codebooks. Around them in the small nondescript room were file cabinets whose drawers yawned open.

Hully snatched a brown, accordion-style folder out of one of the men's hands, before he could dump its contents into the tub of flames. Jardine hopped into the tub and stamped out the fire, like he was mashing grapes into wine.

Sterling had Burroughs train his gun on the four men while the FBI agent patted them down for weapons— they had none. One of the men was the Consulate's treasurer—they were all officials of the consulate.

"Look at this," Hully said, holding up a sheet of typing paper taken from the brown folder. The white sheet bore a detailed sketch of ship locations at Pearl Harbor.

"Where's Morimura?" Burroughs demanded of their prisoners.

"Or should we say 'Yoshikawa'?" Sterling said. "Where is he?"

None of them replied.

But Kita, suddenly helpful, volunteered, "He had a golf match this morning."

Sterling glanced at Burroughs. "Well, he's not in the building."

"Nor is his driver," Kita said.

Jardine took charge of Kita and the others, and Sterling, Burroughs and Hully checked out the Consulate's garage: the Lincoln was gone.

"So we head for the golf course," Sterling said.

"He won't be there," Burroughs said. "He's in hiding."

"Where the hell?"

Burroughs twitched a smile; Hully was nodding as his father said, "I think I know."

And—under a sky momentarily quiet, but still thick with black smoke—they dashed out to the black Ford just as three more carloads of uniformed police, heavily armed, were forming a cordon around the consulate.

# FIFTEEN

## *Retaliation*

In less than half an hour, in a peacetime attack unparalleled in the modern world, Japan had delivered the worst Naval defeat in American history.

Thick black smoke draped Pearl Harbor, where all seven battleships moored at Ford Island had suffered damage, all hit by one or more bombs. In the overturned hull of the *Oklahoma,* most of the crew remained imprisoned, while others were trapped in the capsized *Utah;* rescue efforts in either case were hampered by continual strafing, until the silver planes of the Rising Sun finished their runs.

In the lull that followed the first wave of attack planes, the Americans worked frantically to prepare in the event of another blow—and one was coming: a second wave of 169 fighters and bombers crossed the northern coast of Oahu at 8:40 A.M.

Fifty-four high-level bombers and thirty-one fighters

streaked toward Hickam Field and Kaneohe Naval Air Station and other bases, seeking more American planes on the ground to blow up, often strafing civilian vehicles and residential areas, apparently just for the sheer hell of it. Eighty-one dive bombers prowled for any surviving warships in the harbor, with ships awaiting repairs becoming additional targets—like the flagship *Pennsylvania,* and the destroyers *Downes* and *Cassin,* all in Dry Dock #1.

During this second attack, however, the Japanese pilots met stronger American resistance, and had to deal with billowing black smoke, a cover of their own raid's creation, obscuring their targets. The commander of the second wave of fighters, encountering fiercer ground fire than he'd anticipated, wound up crashing his Zero into a flaming hangar; and efforts to sink the fleeing battleship *Nevada,* to seal off the harbor with a mass of steel, proved unsuccessful.

Small victories, in so large a defeat.

With the exception of the occasional scurrying Oriental, disappearing down an alley or into a doorway, the streets and sidewalks of Chinatown were deserted. The rows of shops and cafés were as abandoned as an Old West ghost town, lacking only tumbleweed; the hustle and bustle of the Aala Market—where Sunday was just another day, any ordinary Sunday, that is—replaced with an eerie silence, deserted stalls filled with fresh fish whose dead faces stared with mute curiosity, as if to say, *Where* is *everybody?*

Under a sky black with storm clouds of war, the

smell of burning could be detected: not the acrid stench of fuel-oil fires from the harbor, but the crackling scorch-scent of refuse disposal, mingled with the unmistakable smell of fear. All around Chinatown, in metal drums or (as at the Consulate) washtubs or in backyard bonfires, *issei* and *nisei* were burning books written in the Japanese language, as well as Rising Sun flags and pictures of the emperor and photos of family members in Japan, even apparel like kimonos and *getta;* they were burying samurai swords and family heirlooms in their backyards—doing their frantic best to nullify any signs of Japanese influence and culture in Honolulu.

Burroughs found in Japanese-dominated Chinatown nothing to confirm the long-held local apprehension that—in the case of war with Nippon—Oahu's Japanese would come charging into *haole* neighborhoods brandishing guns or even samurai swords. Nor was there any sign of them skulking off to plant dynamite satchels and mines under bridges and piers or at military installations and electric lines. And predictions that your own maid, your neighbor's houseboy, the cop on the beat, the farmer down the road, the *nisei* Hawaii Territorial Guard members, would band together against "Americans" (which they of course were themselves) hardly seemed to be materializing.

The distant echo of explosions provided a thunderous backdrop as Ed Burroughs and his son walked by the sampan dock, where the blue boats bobbed, unattended.

"So much for a fifth column," Burroughs said to

Hully, looking around at the desolation, as they approached the small grocery near the Aala Market.

"I'd feel better about this," Hully said, clearly a little nervous, "if Agent Sterling were at our side."

Burroughs held up his palm, where the tiny German automatic nestled. "We'll be fine—Sterling has his own job to do."

"Well, the door's open, anyway," Hully said, and brushed aside the hanging black beads and gestured, politely, for his father to go in first.

The writer stepped inside, Hully right behind him. The wooden storefront was unattended; the place had a curious fragrance, similar to incense—though to Burroughs the unfamiliar scent suggested decay. His son had told him about the shop, but Burroughs was not prepared for how little the "grocery" had to do with his American preconceptions. He glanced around at the walls of shelves lined with jars and baskets of strange herbs, roots, dried seaweed, and other exotica.

"I guess he's out of Ovaltine," Burroughs said dryly.

With his left hand, Burroughs slapped the "Please Ring" bell on the counter, which stretched along the left of the shop.

A door, opposite the beaded one they'd come in, cracked open, apparently from a rear storage area.

"Shop is closed," Yoshio Harada said. Then he recognized them, and the grocer stepped into the storefront, closing the storeroom door behind him. He half bowed. "Burroughs-*san* . . . Burroughs-*san*," he said, acknowledging them both.

"The door was open," Burroughs said, nodding toward the beaded entry. "Sorry to drop by unannounced, but this is an extraordinary morning, wouldn't you say, Mr. Harada?"

Nodding again, the diminutive, trimly mustached man—in a white shirt, grocer's apron, blue trousers, and sandals—shuffled behind the counter at the left; the shelves rising behind him provided a bizarre backdrop of gnarled roots, shark fins and seahorse skeletons.

"A terrible day." Harada was hanging his head. "I am ashamed to be Japanese on this day."

"No kidding?" Burroughs leaned a hand against the counter; his other hand, with the little gun, was behind his back. "I heard you used to have the emperor's picture on display."

Head still bowed, he gestured with both hands, as if disgusted. "I threw it away, many weeks ago. We work so hard to be accepted—to be good American. In one morning, all is undone. I am angry at Japan."

A faraway explosion seemed to punctuate his sentence.

The little grocer shook a fist at the sky. "Dirty Japs!"

"Not bad," Burroughs said, chuckling. "If Weissmuller was as good an actor as you are, Harada, I'd be a happy man."

Harada looked up at the writer, blinking. "Who? What?"

Moving closer to the counter, Hully went into their prepared spiel. "We've just come from the Japanese Consulate, Mr. Harada. General Consul Kita says you and Morimura are buddies."

Harada frowned in apparent confusion. "I know no
one named Morimura."

"How about Yoshikawa?" Burroughs asked, inno-
cently. "A rose by any other name... You see, I
thought, what with bombs dropping and all, you might
be just the guy to help get the vice consul out of the
limelight."

The grocer shook his head. "I know nothing of what
you speak."

"Well," Burroughs said, "to tell you the truth, we
were bluffing. Kita didn't mention your name. Matter
of fact, I doubt Kita even knows your name, unless the
Consulate buys seafood and vegetables from you."

"They do not."

"After all, Kita's not the espionage agent—he'd
likely be kept out of the know, for security reasons.
It's Morimura—that is, Yoshikawa—who's the spy in
the woodpile."

Harada's frown no longer seemed confused, though
his words continued down the path of denial: "I understand none of what you say."

"There's no fifth column in Oahu," Burroughs said
with a grin, which quickly vanished. "But there is a
tiny network of real spies. That radiophone call was a
signal that this Sunday would make a fine morning for
a surprise party. Your niece knew something was up—
more importantly, she knew you were an agent, just
like Otto Kuhn, and Morimura."

Now the mask dropped and a tiny, but very nasty
smile, etched itself on the bland features. "Are these
things you can prove?"

Burroughs shrugged. "Hell, I'll leave that to the FBI." He jerked a thumb at Hully. "My son, here, is the one who really put it together."

Hully said, "I couldn't stop thinking about Morimura bawling Pearl out—she wasn't one of his conquests; he wasn't her type. Why would she even know him? Then it came to me: *through you.* . . ."

"As the grocer making deliveries to the Niumalu," Burroughs said, "you could easily maintain contact with your German 'sleeper' agent. And Pearl was aware of your relationship with both Kuhn and Morimura. After all, she lived with you, up above your shop, before she moved to the Niumalu, so she knew you and Morimura were in league—and she knew or figured out that he was an espionage agent; she even knew his real name. She got wind of something big coming up, and she was going to turn you, and Morimura, in to military intelligence . . . to show her loyalty to America."

"To prove herself," Hully said softly, sadly, "to her boyfriend's father."

Harada held out both empty palms and shook his head, smiling as if this was all too far-fetched, too absurd. "And you think this . . . Morimura . . . killed my niece?"

"No." Burroughs twitched a smile, nodding right at the grocer. "I think you killed her. I *know* you killed her. You confronted her about what you considered her disloyalty, to her family, to Japan, and she told you she was going to Colonel Fielder, to tell him everything. You struck her down, with a goddamn rock, crushed her skull—then Morimura helped cover it up, by calling Kuhn and having him finger the wrong man."

Now the grocer folded his arms and his chin raised; his tone was quietly defiant, now. "I would take offense at these accusations, but they are . . . foolish."

"Oh, there's more. You got to thinking about your niece's close friend, that homosexual musician, and got worried that she may have talked to him, shared what she knew. Or perhaps she bragged to you that she had told Terry Mizuha what she knew, thinking it would protect her, would keep you from harming her. Either way, she was too naive, or maybe too nice a kid, to understand that this is war: that one more casualty, more or less, is nothing to a soldier . . . even if it is his own niece."

Harada said nothing; however, a faint sneer could be detected under the trim mustache.

A slight tremor in his voice, Hully said, "You made an unscheduled, unexpected delivery of seafood to the Niumalu—the day after your niece was murdered! If you had any human compassion or decency, you'd know how suspicious, how wrong that would seem to a normal person."

"You murdered Terry Mizuha at the hotel, probably in his room," Burroughs said, "tossed him in your pickup truck, like another swordfish, and hauled him to the beach."

Hully added, "Though you probably picked up your pal Morimura to help you carry him down that rocky slope to the beach."

Harada smiled, just a little, then looked at each man,

one at a time, with quiet contempt. "You will try to prove this, how?"

Burroughs shrugged. "Like I said, it's not our job to prove it—that's up to the feds, and Detective Jardine. But they're a little busy this morning . . . so I thought I'd help out."

Burroughs brought his hand out from around his back and aimed the Lüger at the grocer's chest.

"What is this?" Harada asked, only his eyes betraying any alarm.

"It's what we Americans call a citizen's arrest."

The backroom door flew open and suddenly Morimura was at Burroughs's side, pressing the nose of a .38 revolver into the writer's neck.

"This is *not* judo," Morimura said. "This is a gun."

The slender, handsome spy wore golf clothes—a checkered sweater vest over a white shirt and knee pants with high checkered socks; well, Kita had said Morimura had a golf date, this morning.

With a sigh, Burroughs set the little Lüger on the counter. The grocer did not take the weapon, rather he reached under the counter and swung out a sawed-off shotgun. Hully and his father exchanged glances—this was not going quite as planned.

"I hope you'll forgive me for eavesdropping," Morimura said, looking a little ridiculous in the golf outfit, though not enough so to take the edge off the weapon he'd stuck in the writer's neck.

"I'll let it go this time," Burroughs said, as the cold steel of the spy's gun dimpled his flesh.

Morimura's expression was smug but his eyes had a

wildness, a fear, in them. "You should write detective stories, Mr. Burroughs. You put the pieces together very well."

The writer looked sideways at his captor. "What now, Morimura? You don't mind if I don't call you 'Yoshikawa'—I'm used to you the other way."

Morimura offered half a smile. "The ineffectual, buffoonish ladies' man, you mean? I must give you credit, Mr. Burroughs—you never did accept that masquerade."

"By any yardstick, buddy, you're no diplomat. You'll face the firing squad, as a spy."

The half smile dissolved into a full scowl. "You're facing a firing squad right now, Mr. Burroughs—something I have no intention of doing."

"What *are* you going to do?" Burroughs did his best to show no fear; and he wasn't afraid for himself—but his son, at his side, that was something again. "You can't just kill us."

"Really?" Morimura laughed softly. "Do you see anyone around to be a witness? Mr. Harada and I will be on the tiny island of Niihau, by nightfall, and a few days later, a submarine will take us to . . . friendlier waters."

Burroughs locked eyes with the spy. "Did you *know*, Morimura? Did you know today was the day?"

The spy smirked, shaking his head. "I suspected—all signs indicated that was the case . . . but it might have been next week, or the next. What was the difference, with your military so obsessed with fighting fifth columnists, and ignoring the real threat?"

Hully was looking at the little grocer, the big hollow eyes of the man's shotgun looking back at him. "How could you do it? How could you kill your own niece?"

Harada's features were impassive, even proud. "She was a traitor."

Hully's eyes were on fire, his nostrils flaring as he said, "She was a beautiful, talented girl, and you murdered her, you heartless son of a bitch!"

Harada shrugged.

Morimura's smile was pursed, like a kiss, and then he said, "Who was it said, 'War is hell'? Whoever that wise man was, he was so right, even if he was an American . . . now if you will please to step in back, in the storeroom."

Burroughs put up his hands and so did Hully, and Morimura reached behind him and pushed the back-room door open with one hand, and with the other he kept the revolver trained on the writer, the grocer keeping a bead on Hully. Morimura motioned with the gun for them to follow him into the back.

The spy did not see Adam Sterling come into the open doorway behind him, and the grocer didn't see the FBI agent in time to warn Morimura, either. With a swift, vicious chop to the base of the neck, Sterling sent Morimura sprawling to the floor, the .38 tumbling from the spy's hands.

Burroughs caught the weapon in midair, and Hully snatched the Lüger from the counter, while Sterling was pointing a .38 revolver of his own at the grocer behind the counter.

Though he had a shotgun in hand, Harada was facing

three guns, all trained on him, from various directions.

"Drop it," Sterling advised. "You can't win this game."

Harada thought that over; then he swung the sawed-off shotgun up and around and under his chin and squeezed both triggers, the explosion shaking everything—and everyone—in the small shop. What had been Harada's head dripped and dribbled and slithered down the weird jars of roots, herbs and skeletons, crawling like strange sea creatures. Then the mostly headless body slid down to the floor and sat, out of sight.

Hully was covering his mouth, horrified. Through his fingers, he said the obvious: "He . . . he took his own life."

"You're going to be seeing a lot of that," Burroughs said, "in the coming days."

Sterling was hauling Morimura to his feet; the dazed spy, his perfect hair askew, looking fairly idiotic in the golf togs, gave the FBI man a bewildered look.

"Judo," Sterling explained.

Less than two hours after it had begun, the sneak air attack on Pearl Harbor was over. The silver planes again receded into specks on the horizon, taking off in varied directions, one more act of deception designed to confuse the enemy as to the attackers' origin point.

The raiders left behind a Pearl Harbor that was a smoldering, twisted landscape of inconceivable devastation. The two pieces of the *Arizona* lay on the bottom of the harbor; the *West Virginia,* too. The *Utah* and

*Oklahoma,* capsized; the *California* sinking; the *Curtiss, Helena,* and *Honolulu* damaged; the *Raleigh* barely afloat; the *Nevada,* the *Vestal,* beached. Fires raged on bomb-damaged ships—the *Maryland,* the *Pennsylvania,* the *Tennessee.*

On Ford Island, the husks of dozens of planes lay in charred disarray, while hangars burned around them. On the oil-pooled surface of the harbor floated debris, much of it human. And along the Oahu shores, the pummeled air bases continued to ooze smoke.

Corpsman attempted, often vainly, to identify bodies and body parts at the Pearl Harbor Naval Hospital. At the base of Alewa Heights, just below the Shuncho-ro teahouse—where the Japanese vice consul had wooed geishas and perpetrated espionage—a makeshift morgue was set up.

The triumph of the Japanese, however, was not complete. Huge fuel tanks, holding millions of barrels of oil, had gone unsullied. The Navy Yard itself, that sprawl of repair facilities and shops, was secure. The Naval ammo depot went untouched, as did the submarine pens. Smaller warships by the score escaped damage; and the raiders had failed to find—much less destroy—the aircraft carriers of the Pacific Fleet.

The greatest miscalculation, of course, was the nature of the attack itself—the sheer villainy of such a peacetime assault. To the Japanese military, this was a glorious day of victory, but just one day—a war, after all, was made of many days.

But December 7, 1941, was not just any day.

Americans would remember it.

# Epilogue

On the afternoon after the attack—in response to a radio request for help from all able-bodied men—Ed and Hully Burroughs were issued Springfield rifles and dispatched to patrol the waterfront in a civilian guard, helping to dig slit trenches along the shore.

With the help of his friend Colonel Kendall Fielder, Burroughs earned the distinction of becoming the oldest American correspondent to cover the Second World War, making three trips to Pacific war zones. He was vocal in his support for Hawaii's Japanese-Americans, though his stereotypical, propagandist portrayal of "Japs" in his WWII novel, *Tarzan and the Foreign Legion,* rivaled that of the Germans in *Tarzan the Untamed.*

Colonel Fielder also became known for championing the rights of Japanese-Americans; possibly he'd been touched in some private way by the deaths of his son and his son's *nisei* fiancée. At any rate, largely due to the efforts of Fielder and a few others—including FBI agent Adam Sterling—99 percent of Hawaii's 160,000 Japanese-Americans remained free, unlike the widespread mainland interments.

Shortly after Pearl Harbor, Burroughs turned his hand to mystery writing, even briefly converting Tarzan into a detective, though without particular success, including a wild crime story entitled "More Fun! More People Killed!" that *The Saturday Evening Post* turned down.

After suffering several heart attacks, Edgar Rice Burroughs died in bed, on March 19, 1950, slumping over the funny papers, which were open to "Tarzan."

Ed Burroughs was very proud of his son Hully, who a few weeks after the Pearl Harbor raid enlisted in the Army Air Corps at Hickam Field; First Lieutenant Hulbert Burroughs went on to be a distinguished aerial combat photographer. Toward the end of the war, Hully married Marion Thrasher; after his father's death, he took the reins of ERB, Inc., working with his brother John Coleman Burroughs to effectively administer the legacy of Edgar Rice Burroughs.

Otto Kuhn and his wife were arrested at a beach house, and imprisoned at the Sand Island Detention Center; Tadeo Yoshikawa (alias Tadashi Morimura) was transported to an interment camp in Arizona and, in August 1942, exchanged for American diplomats held in Japan.

Kuhn and Yoshikawa were two of only a dozen individuals determined to have actively engaged in prewar espionage in Hawaii; grocer Toshio Harada was another. All of them had been sent to Hawaii under false names and/or pretenses; none were representatives of any local fifth column of Japanese-Americans. No such fifth column was ever shown to exist.

Sam Fujimoto fought with the celebrated all-Japanese 442nd Regimental Combat Team, and later graduated from Yale Law School, becoming a successful Honolulu attorney.

Harry Kamana and a smaller version of his band toured the Pacific Theater for the USO.

After the war, Detective John Jardine was instrumental in the cleaning up of police corruption on Oahu; he retired in 1968, died a year later, widely regarded as the finest homicide detective Oahu had ever known.

Both Admiral Kimmel and General Short were forced to retire and a hurried government report in January 1942 branded them with "dereliction of duty." Though a later report absolved them of this charge, the stigma remains, and Admiral Kimmel's son Edward has made a concerted effort to have his father and General Short advanced on the retired lists to their highest wartime ranks of four-star admiral and three-star general.

General Short in his later years spent much time on his garden, cultivating flowers, not actively seeking rehabilitation of his reputation; he died in 1949. Admiral Kimmel—though on December 7, 1941, he seemed to blame himself, at least in part—spent the rest of his life trying to restore his good name, dying of a heart attack in 1968.

The exact circumstances of the attack on Pearl

Harbor, and the reasons for the success of that attack, remain the subject of controversy and debate, involving Congress, the president and media coverage, even sixty years after the fact.

What did the Washington High Command know concerning Japanese intentions and military targets prior to the raid, and why did Washington fail to pass along this information to Kimmel and Short? If the general and admiral had been privy to this information, would they have taken more seriously the Mori message and other evidence of espionage the FBI agent and the creator of Tarzan brought to their attention, the Saturday evening before that fateful Sunday morning?

This Pearl Harbor mystery remains unsolved.

# A Tip of the Panama

This book is a combination of the factual and the fanciful. Details herein of the Japanese attack on Pearl Harbor—including espionage that led up to that attack—are largely factual, although the murder case is a fictional one; and I make no claim, large or small, for this novel as any kind of definitive account of this pivotal event in our history. Any blame for historical and/or geographical inaccuracies is my own, reflecting, I hope, the limitations of conflicting source material.

Like my previous "disaster mysteries," *The Titanic Murders* (1999) and *The Hindenburg Murders* (2000), this novel features a real-life writer as amateur detective. Edgar Rice Burroughs was a great childhood favorite of mine; I was an avid reader of both the Tarzan tales and ERB's science fiction, well into my teens. The narrative technique of separating two protagonists and following the adventures of each in alternating chapters—used in this book—is one I learned from Burroughs. *Tarzan the Untamed,* incidentally, was my favorite of the novels—and the controversy over that "anti-German" title is accurately reported herein.

Burroughs and his son Hulbert were indeed present on Oahu—and living at the Niumalu Hotel—on December 7, 1941; they were, in fact, playing tennis when the bombing began. My fictionalized portrayal of them is based largely upon two wonderful biographies: the massive, seminal *Edgar Rice Burroughs: The Man Who Created Tarzan* (1975) by Irwin Porges; and a book I found as compulsively readable as any Burroughs novel, *Tarzan Forever* (1999) by John Taliaferro. Also helpful were the early Burroughs biographies, *The Big Swingers* (1967) by Robert W. Fenton, and *Edgar Rice Burroughs: Master of Adventure* (1965) by Richard A. Lupoff. So was *Tarzan of the Movies* (1968) by Gabe Esso.

A number of characters in *The Pearl Harbor Murders* are historical figures and appear under their real names, including (of course) General Short and Admiral Kimmel. Colonel Kendall Fielder existed, but the character Bill Fielder is fictional; grocer Yoshio Harada existed, but Pearl Harada is fictional. Adam Sterling is a composite of several FBI agents, one of whom lived at the Niumalu and was friendly with Ed Burroughs. The Kuhns, Colonel Teske (name changed), Tadeo Yoshikawa (a.k.a. Tadashi Morimura), Fred Bivens, George Elliot, Joe Lockard, William Outerbridge, the Morton family, Nagao Kita, and John Jardine are historical figures; Dan Pressman, Jack Stanton, Sam Fujimoto, Terry Mizuha, Frank Kaupiko, and Harry

Kamana are not, although most have real-life counter-parts. Marjorie Petty did visit Oahu shortly before the attack, but (to my knowledge) never dated Hully Burroughs; as a buff of pinup art and artists, I couldn't resist noting the presence in Honolulu of this real, live Petty Girl.

Despite the use of real names and an underlying basis in history, these are all characters in a novel, fictionalized and doing the author's bidding.

My fact-based novels about fictional 1930s/'40s-era Chicago private detective Nathan Heller have required extensive research not unlike what was required here. As usual, my Heller research assistant, George Hagenauer, provided valuable input and came up with research materials on both Pearl Harbor and Edgar Rice Burroughs.

Many books on both Hawaii and the Pearl Harbor attack were consulted, but none was more valuable than *Pearl Harbor Ghosts* (1991) by Thurston Clarke. Mr. Clarke's wonderful book is a vivid picture of Honolulu in 1941 filtered through a modern prism; this work—along with *Tarzan Forever*—provided the spine of my research, and I am indebted to him.

Other Hawaii references consulted include: *All the Best in Hawaii* (1949), Sydney Clark; *Aloha Waikiki* (1985), DeSoto Brown; *Around the World Confidential* (1956), Lee Mortimer; *Detective Jardine: Crimes in Honolulu* (1984), John Jardine with Edward Rohrbough and Bob Krauss; *Hawaii: A Profile* (1940), Merle Colby; *Hawaii Recalls* (1982), DeSoto Brown, Anne Ellett, Gary Giemza; *Hawaii: Restless Rampart*

(1941), Joseph Barber, Jr.; *Hawaiian Tapestry* (1937), Antoinette Withington; *Hawaii!* "... *Wish You Were Here.*" (1994), Ray and Jo Miller; *Hawaiian Yesterdays* (1982), Ray Jerome Baker; *Honolulu-Waikiki Handbook* (1994), J. D. Bisignani; *The Japanese in Hawaii: A Century of Struggle* (1985), Roland Kotani; *Remembering Pearl Harbor* (1984), Michael Slackman; *Roaming Hawaii* (1937), Harry A. Franck; *The View from Diamond Head* (1986), Don Hibbard and David Franzen; *Waikiki Beachboy* (1989), Grady Timmons; and *When You Go to Hawaii* (1930), Townsend Griffiss. The latter—a book I stumbled onto in a Honolulu used-book store while researching the Nathan Heller novel *Damned in Paradise* (1996)—was again particularly useful.

Two especially helpful references were *Pearl Harbor* (1969) by A. J. Barker, and the groundbreaking *Day of Infamy* (1957) by Walter Lord. I also screened the film *Tora! Tora! Tora!* (1970), directed by Richard Fleischer, Toshio Masuda and Kinji Fukasuku. Other valuable references on the attack include: *At Dawn We Slept: The Untold Story of Pearl Harbor* (1981), Gordon W. Prange; *The Broken Seal* (1967), Ladislas Farago; *Dec. 7 1941* (1988), Gordon W. Prange with Donald M. Goldstein and Katherine V. Dillon; *Infamy: Pearl Harbor and its Aftermath* (1982), John Toland; *Long Day's Journey into War: December 7, 1941* (1991), Stanley Weintraub; *Pearl Harbor and the USS Arizona Memorial* (1986), Richard A. Wisniewski; and *Pearl Harbor: The Verdict of History* (1986), Gordon

W. Prange with Donald M. Goldstein and Katherine V. Dillon.

Internet research led me to several useful articles, including "Alewa Teahouse One of the Last of Its Kind" by Rod Ohira (*Honolulu Star-Bulletin*); "The Pearl Harbor Spy" by Wil Deac (thehistorynet.com); and the wonderful overview article "Turning Points: One Sunday in December" by Edward Oxford (*American History* magazine), the single most important research document for my portrayal of the attack itself.

I would like to thank editor Natalee Rosenstein of Berkley Prime Crime for having the foresight to allow me to do this book sooner rather than later—and then to graciously grant me a brief but vital extension; my agent and friend, Dominick Abel; and of course my wife, Barbara Collins, who interrupted her own writing to help me survive various sneak attacks along the way.

# About the Author

Max Allan Collins has earned an unprecedented nine Private Eye Writers of America "Shamus" nominations for his "Nathan Heller" historical thrillers, winning twice (*True Detective,* 1983, and *Stolen Away,* 1991).

A Mystery Writers of America "Edgar" nominee in both fiction and nonfiction categories, Collins has been hailed as "the Renaissance man of mystery fiction." His credits include five suspense-novel series, film criticism, short fiction, songwriting, trading-card sets and movie tie-in novels, including such international bestsellers as *In the Line of Fire, Air Force One,* and *Saving Private Ryan.*

He scripted the internationally syndicated comic strip "Dick Tracy" from 1977 to 1993, is cocreator of the comic-book features "Ms. Tree" and "Mike Danger," and has written the "Batman" comic book and newspaper strip. DreamWorks has bought motion-picture rights to his 1998 graphic novel, *Road to Perdition.*

Working as an independent filmmaker in his native Iowa, he wrote and directed the suspense film *Mommy,* starring Patty McCormack, premiering on Lifetime in 1996, as well as its 1997 sequel, *Mommy's Day.* The recipient of a record four Iowa Motion Picture Awards for screenwriting, he also wrote *The Expert,* a 1995 HBO World Premiere film; and wrote and directed the award-winning documentary *Mike Hammer's Mickey Spillane* (1999) and the innovative feature *Real Time: Siege at Lucas Street Market* (2000).

Collins lives in Muscatine, Iowa, with his wife, writer Barbara Collins, and their teenage son, Nathan.